# NIGHTMARE INSECTS . . .

Ryan tiptoed toward the densest stand of trees, where the heavily leafed branches nearly blocked out the sun and bushes covered the ground. He was sure that was where he'd heard the sounds coming from.

"What are you doing?" Alex demanded.

"Shhh," Ryan cautioned. He reached out and slowly parted the leaves.

He sucked in his breath. A huge creature, at least six feet tall, was looming over him, and he was looking up into large glassy eyes set in a monstrous head. Long antennae whipped the air above it, and huge pincers slashed back and forth like samurai swords. It was a giant ant.

**Read these other BONE CHILLERS from HarperPaperbacks:**

BONE CHILLERS

# ATTACK OF THE KILLER ANTS

## BETSY HAYNES

HarperPaperbacks
*A Division of* HarperCollins*Publishers*

This is a work of fiction. The characters, incidents, and dialogues are products of the author's imagination and are not to be construed as real. Any resemblance to actual events or persons, living or dead, is entirely coincidental.

HarperPaperbacks *A Division of* HarperCollins*Publishers*
10 East 53rd Street, New York, N.Y. 10022

Copyright © 1996 by Betsy Haynes and Daniel Weiss Associates, Inc.

Cover art copyright © 1996 Daniel Weiss Associates, Inc.

First printing: March 1996

Printed in the United States of America

HarperPaperbacks and colophon are trademarks of HarperCollins*Publishers*

❖ 10 9 8 7 6 5 4 3

For the fabulous Street kids from Athens, Georgia:
Paul, David, Kati, and Mandi

# Chapter

1

"**S**chool's out! School's out! Teacher let the weirdos out!" Alex Garvey sang at the top of his lungs.

"And *Ray*-mond's a *weir*-do!" Ryan Miller chimed in.

It was the last day of school, and the kids and teachers from Pine Ridge Elementary were having a picnic to celebrate.

Alex and Ryan had been best friends since the first day of kindergarten, but now they were leaving sixth grade and elementary school behind them forever. Ryan was tall with curly brown hair. Alex was just the opposite—short, chubby, and blond. Raymond was Ryan's nerdy little third-grade brother.

They had finished lunch, and Raymond, also known as Raymond the Brain and Raymond the Pain, was stretched out on the grass. He was propped up on his elbows, watching a parade of ants heading straight for a hunk of bologna and cheese sandwich, which he had carefully placed in a bare spot in the grass.

"Ants always come to a picnic," he said happily. He was the exact image of Ryan, except that he was smaller and there was a gap where he had lost his two front baby teeth.

"Don't you have enough fun with your ant farm at home? Everybody's looking at you," Ryan complained. He hated the way Raymond always embarrassed him in front of his friends.

"Don't worry, Ryan. I'll still play with you even if your little brother is a weirdo," Alex said, grinning wickedly.

Raymond ignored both of them, picking up an ant at the back of the line and setting it squarely on a piece of bread. "Go ahead and eat," he coaxed.

"Yum!" Ryan exclaimed. He grabbed the ant off the bread and popped the ant into his mouth.

"Gross!" Raymond cried. "Let it go!"

Ryan put his face up close to his brother and spit the ant out onto the grass near where Raymond was lying. Then Ryan and Alex doubled over with laughter.

Just then Dolph Kruger stomped by. Dolph was the same age as Ryan and Alex, but he looked like a teenager. He was tough, too, and when he said something, everybody listened. Naturally he had something to say right then.

"Hey, everybody! Look at Ryan's geeky little brother. He's playing with ants!" Dolph threw back his head and roared.

Now everybody was looking at Raymond, and at Ryan, who could feel his face turning a fiery shade of red.

Ryan had to admit it, Raymond *was* a geek. And he wasn't called Raymond the Brain for nothing. He was a third-grade genius and a walking encyclopedia of information about everything that crawled, walked on four legs, or flew.

In addition to his ant farm, he had three butterfly cocoons hanging on his bedroom curtain and a hamster that rolled all over the house in a plastic ball. And Raymond the Brainy Pain loved to tag along with Ryan and Alex and spout off all his boring knowledge.

Dolph Kruger wasn't finished yet. He poked Ryan's shoulder with a stubby finger.

"Hey, Ryan. Do you play with ants, too?"

"You're so funny," Ryan muttered, and turned away. But instead of discouraging Dolph, it only egged him on.

"Yeah, do you feed them with an itty-bitty teaspoon? And dress them up in teensy-weensy clothes?" He was laughing so hard he had to wipe his watery eyes.

Other kids were laughing, too. It was all Raymond's fault. Ryan wanted to die.

He sneered at Dolph. No matter whose fault it was, he couldn't let the big bully get away with a thing like that.

"Yeah, I play with ants," he said sarcastically. "Like this."

He picked up one of the ants feasting on Raymond's sandwich and stuck it under Dolph's nose, making his eyes cross. Using the fingers of his other hand like tweezers, Ryan pulled off each of the ant's six legs. "See?" he said triumphantly, and tossed the ant into the grass.

Dolph gave him a disgusted look and walked away. But Ryan's victory was short-lived. Something crashed hard into his stomach. It was Raymond's fist.

"Why'd you do that, you big glob of snot?" Raymond shouted. "You hurt that ant! You probably killed him! What'd he ever do to you?"

"It was just a stupid ant," Ryan muttered. "What's your problem?"

Raymond bent over and picked up the ant, holding the lifeless bug out on the tip of his finger. "Look what you did!" he cried, punching at Ryan again.

Ryan dodged the punch and jabbed back at Raymond, missing him by a hair. "So what, weirdo?"

Alex had been watching quietly. Now he got an impish grin on his face and called out gleefully, "Look at this, Raymond." He began jumping up and down on the hunk of sandwich that was now almost solid black with ants. He smushed ants and smeared bologna and cheese and bread around in the grass. A few ants escaped, scattering in every direction.

Raymond clenched his fists and let out an ear-splitting scream.

Mr. Fredd, the fifth-grade teacher, came running over. "Boys! What's going on? Are you okay, Raymond?"

"It's them!" Raymond cried, pointing an accusing finger at Ryan and Alex. "They're killing ants!"

Mr. Fredd's look of alarm slowly sagged into disinterest. "They're *what?*"

"They're stomping ants and killing them and pulling their legs off and stuff. Make them stop!"

"Raymond, I know you like bugs," Mr. Fredd began patiently, "but—"

"You don't understand about ants," Raymond interrupted. "They're intelligent. I mean, really smart! They can talk to each other with their feelers. And they help each other out and share food and everything, just like humans."

Ryan noticed with relief that a fight had broken out among some fourth-grade boys, and Mr. Fredd was darting anxious glances in that direction.

"That's interesting, Raymond. You'll have to tell me all about it sometime. Right now I have to see what's going on over there." He hurried off toward the crowd that was gathering around the brawling boys.

"They *are* smart," Raymond muttered to himself. "They dig underground cities and have real cemeteries outside their anthills where they bury dead ants."

"Hey, Raymond. Come on, let's see how smart they really are," Alex suggested. He still had that wicked gleam in his eyes, and Ryan knew he was up to something.

Alex dropped to his knees and scooped a shallow hole in the dirt. Then he grabbed a can of soda off a nearby picnic table and dumped it into the hole.

"What are you doing?" Raymond asked, watching the soda bubble and fizz.

Alex picked three or four ants out of the grass, and before Raymond could figure out what was going on, Alex dropped them into the liquid.

"Hey, a swimming pool for ants!" Ryan shouted.

"Yeah, do you think these little buggers know how to swim?" Alex laughed, dropping two more ants in with the others.

Ryan picked through the grass, adding three more.

Raymond watched in silence, tears streaming down his face, as each ant struggled for several seconds and then lay still, floating like pond scum on the surface of a pool.

Ryan spotted two more ants trying to make a fast getaway by scurrying through the grass.

"Aha!" he cried, picking up one in each hand. "Let's see if they'll talk to each other." He drew his hands together slowly until the ants were facing each other, almost touching.

Suddenly they began waving their antennae like crazy, reaching out and trying to touch each other. Ryan inched them a little closer.

"Look at that!" Alex shouted when the two ants clasped each other's feelers. "They're talking, just like Raymond said. Hey, Raymond. Come and watch these two ants talk!"

Raymond marched toward Ryan with a pouty look on his face. "You put those ants down right now!" he demanded.

He swiped at Ryan, but Ryan was too fast for him.

Ryan held the ants above his head, higher

than Raymond could reach. "Listen to them talking, Raymond. What do you think they're saying?"

Tears flooded Raymond's eyes again as he looked up helplessly at the ants.

Ryan felt a sudden stab of guilt at the misery on his little brother's face. Sometimes he wished it weren't so much fun to tease the nerdy little kid. But wasn't that what big brothers were for?

"Hey, Raymond, listen," he said, touching the ants together again.

"Yeah, but they're talking way too loud," said Alex. He pulled the antennae off both ants' heads and smiled with satisfaction. "There. That's better."

Raymond's face was a deep shade of purple, and he looked as if he were about to burst. "I'm going *home!* And I'm going to *tell!*" he said, spinning around and heading for the park exit.

"Raymond, wait!" Ryan called, but Raymond marched straight through the gate. "Come on, Alex. He's probably going home, but Mom and Dad will kill me if I let him go on his own."

Ryan looked around for Mr. Fredd and was surprised to see that while he and Alex had been teasing Raymond, most of the other kids had left the park.

"Mr. Fredd," he called when he spotted his teacher, "we're going now."

"Bye, boys," Mr. Fredd called back. "Have a good summer."

Ryan grabbed his backpack and the junk he had cleaned out of his desk and headed for the gate. When he caught Raymond, he would beat him to a pulp for running off. He might even let Alex help.

When he got to the street, he looked both ways, but there was no Raymond. Neat rows of houses lined the deserted street, which dead-ended at the woods.

"Where'd he go?" asked Alex. "He couldn't have gotten away that fast. His legs are too short."

Ryan's heart was thumping. "Yeah, he's got to be around here somewhere."

"You think that instead of going home, he's hiding from us?" Alex asked.

Ryan nodded slowly. He'd been thinking the same thing, and he had a feeling he knew exactly where Raymond the Brainy Pain would go—out where he could talk to his precious ants and butterflies and spiders. Ryan glanced toward the woods and shuddered.

Hanging out there with his whole class was one thing, but being alone in the woods was creepy. He had heard so many stories about kids wandering away from the road and never finding it again. Still, he couldn't let anything happen to his little brother.

"Come on, Alex. Let's go get him."

# Chapter

yan led the way, following a path into the woods. His fists were clenched and his jaw was set with determination.

"Raymond!" he called out at the top of his lungs. When they reached the end of the path, he stared into the mass of towering trees and tangled undergrowth. "Raymond, stop goofing around. Everyone's gone home."

Raymond didn't answer, and Ryan glanced nervously over his shoulder. The foliage seemed to be closing in behind them.

"Maybe he didn't come in here after all," Alex said hopefully. "Maybe he went on home, like he said."

"Naw, he's in here all right," Ryan assured him. "I know him, remember? He's getting revenge on us for what we did to the ants. Only we have to find him before he gets lost."

"How do you know he didn't go home so he could show off his report card before you get there?" Alex asked.

Ryan thought a minute. Naturally Raymond the Brain got straight A's. And Ryan always got mediocre grades.

"Maybe," Ryan said slowly. "He might have gone running to Mom and Dad to show off." If that was true, he wouldn't have to spend another minute in these spooky woods.

Then something else occurred to him. "But you know what that'll mean when they see mine. I'll be *road kill*. I'll bet that's how he's going to get his revenge."

Suddenly Ryan heard a crashing sound up ahead. Raymond was racing through the trees and leaping from rock to rock. Grinning back over his shoulder at Ryan and Alex, he grabbed a loose vine and swung out over the forest floor like Tarzan. "Ahh-*eee*-ahh-*eee*-ahh-*eee*-ahh!"

Then he darted off, ducking out of sight in the underbrush.

"There he is! After him!" Ryan yelled.

The boys plowed through the woods, dodging branches and leaping over moss-covered logs.

"I see him!" Alex yelled a couple of minutes later. "Look! He's heading over that way!"

Ryan nodded and made a quick left off the path. He gulped in air and pumped his legs even harder. He was getting madder at Raymond by the minute. The little brat was running deeper into the woods.

"Stop, Raymond!" he yelled. "I mean it. You're gonna get it. Do you hear me?"

If Raymond heard, he didn't let on. Instead, he disappeared again, this time into a patch of pines.

Ryan staggered to a stop. He was panting hard, and he had a ripping pain in his side. But he couldn't give up. He'd catch Raymond and drag him home by the scruff of the neck if that was what it took.

Alex was looking around, frowning.

"What's the matter?" Ryan asked.

"I don't hear him anymore," Alex replied.

Ryan shrugged. "He's probably lying low."

Alex nodded. "Yeah, watching us and laughing his head off."

Ryan glanced around at the deepening shadows. It was getting late. And the woods were strangely silent. No birds were singing, and the gentle croaking of the forest insects had stopped.

Alex must have felt the same way. "Let's go back," he urged. "It's getting spooky in here. Besides, Raymond's probably long gone by now."

Ryan hesitated. "But what if he isn't?" he argued. "What if it gets dark and he can't find his way out?"

"Yeah," Alex said, rubbing his hands together in anticipation. "And what if he gets eaten by a bear or something? Hee hee hee."

"Cut it out, Alex," Ryan grumbled. "You know I'm supposed to take care of the little jerk." He was actually feeling more worried about Raymond than angry. What if something really *had* happened to him? Alex didn't have a brother, so he didn't understand.

Suddenly Alex's hand shot out and grabbed Ryan's arm. "Listen!" he said.

Ryan listened, but he didn't hear a thing. He started to move on, but Alex squeezed his arm tighter.

"Didn't you hear it? There! I just heard it again!" Alex's eyes were wide with fright.

Ryan listened harder and stared into the tangle of trees. This time he made out a faint rhythmic scuffling noise. It sounded as if someone was walking softly over the pine needles and dead leaves that carpeted the forest floor.

"It's Raymond," he whispered. "He thinks he's sneaking up on us. Act like you don't hear him."

Alex grinned. "Got it," he whispered back, and nudged Ryan with his elbow. Then in a loud voice he said, "We're never gonna find Raymond. I guess he's too smart for us."

"Right," Ryan answered, grinning back. "I guess that's why he gets straight A's in school. We might as well give up and go home."

Behind them a twig snapped.

Ryan winked at Alex and a smile spread across his face. It was all he could do to keep from laughing out loud. It was working. The little brat actually thought he was fooling them. That was okay, Ryan thought. He and Alex would lead Raymond toward home and grab him at the edge of the woods. It would be easy.

Ryan picked a path through the trees, hoping it would take them back to the park, where they had entered the woods. He looked around uneasily. He didn't know the woods very well— at least not as well as Raymond did. Nothing looked familiar. He could hear the steady crunch of footsteps behind him.

As long as Raymond was so close, he probably didn't have to worry about his little brother's getting lost, he decided. *Except that now I'm lost,* he thought, trying to hold down his panic.

"Are you sure you know where you're going?" Alex asked after a while.

Ryan looked at Alex sheepishly. He knew he should admit that he was lost. He noticed that the footsteps behind him had stopped, too.

He put his finger to his lips, signaling for Alex to be quiet. Then he took two quick steps, being sure to make plenty of noise. He waited. Then he heard it. *Crunch. Crunch.* He took two more steps and stopped.

When Ryan stopped, the footsteps stopped, too.

Ryan sighed in disgust. "Raymond Miller, quit fooling around!" he shouted angrily. "I know you're back there."

Raymond didn't answer.

"You think you're pretty cute, don't you?" Ryan went on.

"Hey, what if it isn't Raymond?" Alex asked in alarm.

"It's Raymond, all right," Ryan muttered. He slowly scanned the silent trees, but he couldn't see any sign of his little brother. He peered into the dense leaves, expecting to see another pair of eyes peering back at him.

Nothing.

*Raymond must be waiting,* Ryan thought. *He's hanging back and waiting for us to make another move. He'll jump out at us and yell "boo" or something. The little idiot must really think he'll scare us.*

Ryan smiled to himself and tiptoed toward the densest stand of trees, where the heavily leafed branches nearly blocked out the sun and thick bushes covered the ground. He was sure that was where he'd heard the sounds coming from. He wasn't going to let Raymond have that kind of satisfaction. He'd get the nerdy little brat first.

"What are you doing?" Alex demanded.

"Shhh," cautioned Ryan. He reached out and slowly parted the leaves. "Raymo—"

Ryan sucked in his breath. To his horror, a huge creature, at least six feet tall, was looming over him. Ryan was looking up into large, glassy eyes set in a monstrous head. Long antennae whipped the air above it, and huge pincers slashed back and forth like samurai swords. It was a giant ant.

Behind him, he heard Alex scream. At the same instant he felt ropelike tentacles wrap around him and lift him slowly into the air.

# Chapter

"**P**ut me down!" Ryan shrieked. He tugged frantically at the ant's forelegs, which bound him like steel cables. The ant held him high above its head, and he tried desperately to loosen its grasp. His heart pounded in terror.

But the ant gripped him more tightly than ever, holding him so that he was on his back, facing up into the trees.

Instantly more giant ants swarmed around him, touching him all over with their feelers and nodding to each other as if they were approving a slab of ribs for a barbecue. He cringed and tried to shrink away from their antennae, but there was nowhere to retreat.

20

"Alex!" he cried as a new wave of terror swept over him. "Help!"

"They've got me too!" Alex croaked. "What are we going to do?"

Ryan's mind raced wildly. "Raymond!" he called at the top of his lungs. "If you can hear me, go get help!"

He had no idea if Raymond had heard him, but if he had, surely he would go get their dad or maybe the police. He couldn't just leave them.

The ants were beginning to move. Ryan tilted his head back so that he could see what they were doing, even though everything looked upside down. He was lying feet forward, so he could see only what was behind him.

The ants walked in a line, single file. Alex had been captured by the lead ant, and Ryan was right behind him, high above the head of the ant that was second in line.

Ryan listened to the rustling sounds the ants' feet made as they walked across the leaf-carpeted forest floor. His heart almost stopped. It was the same sound of footsteps he had heard when he thought Raymond was following him and Alex. It hadn't been Raymond after all.

They had been stalked through the woods by giant ants!

*So where is Raymond right now?* he wondered frantically. Had they captured him, too? Maybe eaten him or done something terrible to him?

Tears stung Ryan's eyes. He couldn't think like that. At least not right at that moment. He had to believe that Raymond had heard his cry for help and was running home that very instant.

The ants were marching through the trees at a steady cadence, and he swayed gently back and forth as they walked. They were heading deeper and deeper into the shadowy forest, and Ryan realized with a start that they were carrying him to a part of the woods where he'd never been before.

Tattered cobwebs hung from the dark trees like forgotten laundry. Birds called to each other in low, mournful tones. Here and there patches of light broke through the foliage and stabbed the dark ground like laser beams.

Still the ants marched on, farther and farther away from anything that looked familiar. Even if he and Alex could escape from the ants, how could they ever find their way home?

Suddenly the blood rushed to Ryan's head. At first he couldn't figure out why. Then it dawned on him that they must be going uphill! The ants were moving more slowly now, as if it was hard work to make their way up the steep embankment.

Ryan tilted his head as far back as he could to try to see where they had been. Beneath the ants' feet the dirt looked as if it had been patted smooth. The trees were all behind them now as they climbed and climbed. They stopped when they reached the crest of the gigantic hill and the terrain leveled off.

Slowly Ryan felt himself being lowered to the ground. The ant stood him upright in front of a huge crater. Alex was standing next to him, his eyes wide with fright.

The ants had formed a circle around the pit. Suddenly Ryan understood. He looked around frantically.

"Alex!" he screamed. "This is an anthill!" The idea exploded into his mind like a firecracker.

Alex opened his mouth to answer, but the ant

that had been carrying him gave him a shove, sending him tumbling into the crater.

Ryan gasped. The last thing he saw of Alex was the tread on the bottoms of his sneakers as he sank into the darkness and disappeared.

# Chapter

Ryan stared at the dark hole in horror. It was the entrance to an anthill the size of a two-story building, and Alex had just been pushed into it.

Ryan's heart pounded like a jackhammer inside his chest. He stared at the hole. It was about four feet in diameter, perfectly round, and *perfectly silent.*

Suddenly he caught a glimpse out of the corner of his eye of a whiplike arm shooting out from behind him. It hung poised in the air above his head like a snake about to strike.

Trembling in terror, Ryan tried to duck. But in the blink of an eye it lunged forward and gave him a gigantic shove toward the dark opening in the earth.

He heard someone scream and knew it must be himself. He was rolling downward, tumbling headlong into pitch blackness.

Dirt filled his mouth. It stung his eyes as he fell. He plunged head over heels, gathering speed as he careened into the black emptiness below.

Suddenly he slammed to a stop against a wall of damp earth. Ryan shook his head, trying to clear his mind. Was this really happening? Had he been pushed down a giant anthill by an ant that was six feet tall? Feebly he reached out a hand. He was on his side, lying against a dirt wall somewhere deep inside the earth.

Ryan swallowed hard and opened his eyes as wide as he could, trying to see through the blackness.

Suddenly he remembered Alex.

"Alex!" he screamed. "Where are you? Answer me!"

There was no sound except the drumbeat of his own pulse pounding in his head.

Then he heard something. A tiny whisper.

"Over here."

"Alex? Is that you? Where?" he whispered back.

"Yes," came the faint reply. "Come here, but be careful."

Ryan crawled toward the sound of Alex's voice. His eyes were starting to adjust to the darkness, and he could see the shadowy outline of an underground tunnel.

"Keep talking so I can find you," he said softly.

"Over here," Alex called.

Ryan rounded a bend. Far above him, he could make out a faint patch of light. He squinted upward and gasped.

The opening! It looked miles and miles away. Could he have fallen that far?

Then he saw Alex, sitting on a sort of ledge where the tunnel dropped off sharply into abysmal blackness.

He looked toward the light again and whistled low. The path back up to the top was long and almost straight up and down.

Turning back to Alex, he asked anxiously, "Are you okay?"

Alex nodded.

"Me too," said Ryan. "At least I think I am."
He felt a throbbing in his ankle, but he didn't
want Alex to know. He was scared enough
already. Ryan glanced back up at the pinpoint of
light as panic flooded him once more. "How are
we gonna get out of here?" he wailed.

"Maybe we aren't," Alex whispered, his voice
quivery. "Maybe we're trapped here forever and
nobody will ever find us. They'll look for a while
and then give up, and we'll be stuck—"

"Don't say that!" Ryan huffed, interrupting
Alex. "Of course we're going to get home. All
we have to do is figure out how, that's all."

Ryan gave his friend a nervous glance. He
could see horror written all over Alex's face. He
had to stay calm! He took a deep breath and
exhaled slowly. It made him feel a little better,
but not much.

He pictured the giant ants in his mind: the
way their bodies were split into three sections,
the six spindly legs. Their mouths had been like
big pincers—just like the ants in Raymond's ant
farm, only bigger. *Just like the ants we tortured
at the picnic,* he thought, and shuddered.

His heart was pounding again, banging against his ribs like a loose shutter in a windstorm. All of his senses told him it couldn't be true.

But he had to accept it. The ants were real.

Ryan wanted to cry. He wanted to throw back his head and wail. But he knew it wouldn't do any good. At least he and Alex were alone in the terrible darkness. The ants were still outside, on the top of the hill.

What could the giant insects possibly be planning? He stared up in misery at the pinhole of light that was his only escape.

Suddenly he heard the sound of marching feet, and the light above them was blotted out. Ryan clutched Alex, and the two boys clung together in terror as the column of marching ants headed down the long passageway from above.

"They're coming," Alex whispered. "They're coming to get us!"

# Chapter

"**G**et down," Ryan whispered. He was pressing into the loose earth of the dirt wall, and he motioned for Alex to do the same. "Maybe they won't see us and they'll go right on by. Then we can try to climb out of here."

Alex nodded and shrank into the darkness beside Ryan.

The ants were coming closer. They reminded Ryan of a column of soldiers. Or maybe a firing squad, off to get a condemned prisoner and carry out the sentence. He cringed in terror as they marched straight toward him and Alex with their feelers out in front of them, sweeping the air.

"They're looking for us," Alex squeaked.

"Shhh," Ryan cautioned. He held his breath as the marching ants came within feeling distance. The insects passed them and continued feeling their way through the darkness.

"Come on! Let's get out of here!" Ryan shrieked as soon as the last ant had disappeared. "It won't take long for them to realize they've missed us and come back."

He leaped to his feet and lunged upward toward the speck of light, scratching at the dirt as he scrambled toward freedom. Alex was beside him, panting hard as he struggled to climb up the incline, too.

Ryan kicked at the soft soil, trying to find footholds. His hands flailed at the dirt over his head, searching for rocks or clods of earth to use as anchors.

It was no use. It all crumbled and fell away. No matter how hard they tried to climb, they slid back down to the bottom.

As Ryan stopped to catch his breath, he felt something hard and ropelike wrap around his right leg.

They were back!

Another tentacle twined around his left arm and a third one belted itself around his middle. He gasped as he was suddenly lifted high in the air. He knew what was happening, but he was helpless to stop the ant from carrying him down deeper into the darkness.

"No!" he cried. "Alex! Keep going! Go for help!"

But when he looked at Alex, his friend's eyes were wild with fright, and he was fighting off the long, snaky legs of another monster ant.

"Let go of me!" Ryan screamed as he yanked and tugged, but he couldn't break loose. "*Please,* just let me go home!"

His eyes were now adjusted to his shadowy world, and he became aware that he was in a giant labyrinth, being carried farther and farther downward through a maze of rooms and tunnels. Thoughts churned in his mind. How deep did the tunnel go?

Ryan tried to picture Raymond's ant farm. It had sat on his nerdy little brother's windowsill for ages, but he had scarcely paid any attention to it. Now he strained to remember the twists and turns of the tunnels inside the glass.

*What difference does it make what that stupid ant farm looked like? It won't help us get out of here,* he realized.

He tried to fight down the tears that were clogging his throat and stinging his eyes. He wanted to be home, safe in his own room. He wanted to hear his parents scolding him about his D+ in English. He even wanted to play with nerdy Raymond again!

Suddenly he was falling. The ant had dropped him, and he landed hard. He quickly rolled over. The monstrous face of the ant loomed just above him.

A pair of large, bulbous eyes stared at him from the sides of the insect's head. Huge pincer jaws moved slowly from side to side as the ant snipped the air hungrily.

But even more frightening was the pair of long antennae, which protruded from the lower part of the creature's head. Ryan froze in terror as the antennae wiggled and reached around, softly touching his face. The ant's feelers stroked his arms and ran down along his sides and the full length of his legs.

Ryan's skin was crawling with goose bumps. *What if it's sizing me up for a meal?* he thought.

He was still staring up at the hideous monster when Alex crashed down beside him. A second ant joined Ryan's captor. The two insects stood over the boys for a moment and then slowly turned and moved away, disappearing into the dusky tunnel.

Alex stared after them, dazed. Then he saw Ryan, and relief flooded his face. "Where are we?" he whispered.

"How should I know?" Ryan whispered back. "Somewhere even deeper down in the anthill."

Neither boy said anything for a moment. Then Ryan looked around nervously. "What do you think they want with us?" he asked in a husky voice. "They wouldn't—" He stopped.

"Wouldn't what?" Alex asked fearfully.

*"Eat us,"* whispered Ryan. "They wouldn't do that . . . would they?"

# Chapter

**R**yan and Alex sat together on the dirt floor of the tunnel in miserable silence. They could hear the scratching sounds of insects busily scurrying back and forth through the long passageways. Strange crunching noises came through the walls from a nearby chamber.

"There must be hundreds of 'em," Alex said.

Ryan frowned. "More than that," he said. "Thousands. Maybe even millions in just one colony. At least that's what Raymond says."

"What does Raymond say they do down here?" Alex asked warily.

Ryan shrugged. "I can't remember. I never really listened to much of what he said."

"Well, try," pleaded Alex. "It might help us figure out how to get out of here."

Ryan took a deep breath, smelling the damp, earth-scented air, and thought hard. Raymond was always running off at the mouth about something, but Ryan usually tried to tune him out.

"I remember him saying something about . . . about ant colonies having queens that did nothing but have babies, and a lot of workers, who took care of everything else. Or was that bees instead of ants?"

"I think it's ants, too," Alex said. "I know that much. The workers leave the hill to look for food, and they dig out the tunnels and the little rooms where they store food and stuff."

"Of course. Everybody knows that," Ryan huffed.

"Keep on thinking," Alex urged. "Did Raymond tell you anything else?"

"Like what?" Ryan asked.

"I don't know. If I did, we'd be outta here by now," Alex said.

Ryan bit back the angry words that came to his lips. This was no time for fighting. He and

Alex needed each other if they were ever going to escape.

Ryan looked around the room. It was carved out of the dirt and shaped like a cave, long and narrow with a low ceiling. He had seen pictures of anthills dozens of times, and this room looked exactly like the ones in the pictures.

"I guess we should try to sneak out of here while we have the chance," he said.

"You mean go look around?" Alex asked in amazement.

"Yeah, and maybe find the way out," Ryan said, even though he wasn't sure he liked the idea that much himself.

"Are you crazy?" Alex burst out. "What if one of those big buggers is hanging around outside the door? And what if it takes one look at us and decides it's lunchtime?"

"You got a better idea?" Ryan growled.

Alex shook his head.

"We can't just sit here. We have to do something," Ryan said. "They could come back for us any minute. Besides, what if Raymond went back to the house and got Dad or the police? The nearer we are to the entrance, the better our chances of being rescued."

"Okay, okay. Let's go," Alex muttered.

Ryan's heart was thumping fast. He and Alex crept cautiously toward the doorway of their little cave. Everything was quiet for the moment.

Ryan took a deep breath and let it out slowly. Maybe they would be able to sneak through the maze of tunnels to the entrance after all. The giant insects were creepy, but how smart could they be?

That thought made him feel a little better. Of course they could outsmart a bunch of bugs. He didn't know why he'd been so scared. All it would take was a little brain power.

"Come on, let's hurry up. I'm starved, and when I get home I'm going to have one mega snack," he said confidently.

"Yeah, I'm hungry, too," Alex admitted.

They were almost to the door when a giant shadow loomed in the entrance.

Both boys flattened themselves against the wall of the chamber and held their breath as an ant made its way inside.

The ant stopped and waved its antennae

around the middle of the room. Finding nothing, it started running them along the walls. Ryan and Alex stood cringing in terror. The huge feelers skittered along their wall, sending showers of fine dirt billowing into the air and cascading onto the floor. It was searching for the boys!

All of a sudden Ryan felt a sneeze coming on.

*Oh, no!* he thought. He couldn't sneeze! The ant would be sure to find them. And it might signal a hundred ants to descend on them. Surely they'd be eaten if that happened. But the dust was tickling his nose and making it hard to breathe.

Ryan pinched the bridge of his nose to hold the sneeze inside. Raymond always did that when he was trying not to sneeze, but Ryan couldn't remember if it worked.

His head felt like a big balloon, blowing up bigger and bigger. "Ahhh— Ahhh—"

Alex glanced at Ryan, his eyes wide with terror. He pointed to the ant that was inching closer and closer as it felt along the wall.

Ryan nodded, but there was nothing he could do. The sneeze grew and grew until . . .

"Ahhh— Ahhh— Ahhh-*choo!*" The sneeze exploded like a dynamite charge.

The huge ant stiffened to attention, and its antennae froze in midair.

Ryan trembled as the bug swung around slowly in his and Alex's direction. The antennae began moving again, reaching out and feeling the air until one patted Ryan's face. Then the ant lumbered toward the cowering boys.

Ryan crouched as low as he could, but it didn't help. He could feel the blood drain from his face as the giant ant once more ran its feelers along his body. Then it moved to Alex, repeating the same routine. It was standing directly in front of them. Ryan knew they were trapped.

The monster rose on its back legs and waved all four front legs in the air. Then, hovering menacingly over Ryan and Alex, its giant pincers slowly began to open.

Ryan knew they weren't just trapped. They were *doomed!*

# Chapter

7

The ant wrapped one steely tentacle around Ryan's arm and one around Alex's and began dragging them out into the tunnel. Ryan stiffened his legs and tried to use his feet like brakes, but it didn't work. The ant was too strong. He pulled them along the passageway like two pieces of grass.

Ryan tried to see which path they were taking, but it was impossible. Tunnels intersected other tunnels and made turns to the right and turns to the left. Little rooms opened up all along the maze. He and Alex would never be able to find their way out on their own.

Suddenly the big insect pulled them into a

huge room filled with dozens of ants. They were milling around and talking to each other by rubbing their antennae together. Gradually the shuffling feet grew still, and the ants unclasped each other's antennae.

"What's happening?" Alex whispered.

All the ants had turned to face the boys now, and he knew something awful was about to happen.

For a moment nothing in the room stirred. Then one ant stepped forward. It was slightly bigger than the others. The shell-like covering on its body looked worn and scratched, and there was a triangular chip in one of its pincers. Ryan guessed that it was the oldest ant in the room, and he knew immediately that it was in charge.

Placing a long, ropelike leg on each of the boys' heads, it began waving its antennae excitedly.

The next thing Ryan knew, two ants rushed forward and grabbed him, wrestling him down and pinning him spread-eagled on the ground.

"Help!" he cried, even though he knew there was no one to help him. Alex was on the floor beside him, pinned there by two more ants. They were both completely helpless!

The tall ant waved its antennae again, and there was a sudden rush as the other ants stampeded toward the boys.

"Oof!" cried Ryan as one of the ants landed on his chest and began jumping up and down.

"Let go of my leg!" shouted Alex.

At that same instant, Ryan felt a hard tug on his own leg. Ants were all over him now. They were jumping on his chest. They were pulling on his arms. His legs. Even his ears!

*"Aaaaaiiiieeee!"* he screamed.

But the ants kept pounding on him. They snatched and grabbed and pulled. They jerked his arms and legs almost out of their sockets. They twisted his ears painfully. They stamped on him mercilessly, until he knew his chest and sides had to be black and blue.

Then, as quickly as the ants had begun jumping on Ryan and Alex, they retreated. One by one they backed slowly away and formed a circle around the exhausted boys.

Ryan wasn't sure whether to feel relieved or even more frightened. The ants looked like vultures, their huge pincers moving side to side hungrily.

The bigger ant took command again, and Ryan felt himself being lifted into the air and carried back into the tunnel.

"Where are they taking us this time?" Alex asked in a panicky voice. "They're going to kill us, aren't they? And eat us!"

Ryan fought down his own panic. "Don't say that, Alex! We're still alive, aren't we?"

"Yeah, but—" Alex's voice broke off. Then he shouted, "Oh, no! No!"

There was a loud splash, and then Ryan felt himself airborne. He hurtled through the air like a rocket, arcing high, and then plunged headfirst into a murky pool. He came up sputtering. Beside him, Alex flailed wildly in the water.

"What are they trying to do? Drown us?" Alex shouted.

Suddenly Ryan understood. "That's it!" he shouted back as he dog-paddled. "Keep your head above water and swim, Alex. Show them how smart you are."

Alex frowned but started dog-paddling also.

44

"What are you talking about? They're serious. They want to drown us."

"Of course they do, because that's what we did to the ants in the park. And we pulled their legs off, too. Remember? And stomped on them. That's what they were doing to us. Now they're trying to drown us."

Alex got an incredulous look on his face. "Wow! You're right. But the ants aren't strong enough to keep us prisoner or to pull off our legs, or heavy enough to stomp us to death. And they're not coming in after us now because they can't swim!"

"Exactly," Ryan said, looking at the ants ringing the water. Some of them were making conversation with their feelers. Others looked out across the water at the boys, but none of them came in.

*This pond must be the underground reservoir that holds the drinking water for the ant city,* he realized. *We're safe as long as we stay here.*

The boys swam to the center of the pond and treaded water. The ants were gathered all around the shores of the pond.

"We can't stay in here forever," Alex said after a few minutes. "I'm getting tired. And *hungry!*"

"Me too," Ryan admitted. His body ached from the beating he'd taken from the ants. His arms and legs felt like lead weights in the foul-smelling water. He wasn't sure how much longer he could hold out.

Suddenly he noticed activity onshore. The ants were lashing tree branches together with vines. "Alex, look!" he shouted. "They're making a raft."

"Oh, no," Alex said. "They're coming after us!"

A raft holding two huge ants pushed away from the edge of the pond. Ryan started to swim to the other side. He had to move faster than they did, he thought. But he was getting so tired.

Just one more stroke, he told himself. And then another. His arms were getting much too heavy to raise over his head. His eyelids were getting heavy, too. His brain was turning to mush. It was just too hard.

Finally he had to stop trying. He felt himself softly drifting.

# Chapter

When Ryan awoke he was crumpled in a heap on the dirt floor of another small room in the anthill. His clothes were soaked, and his body ached. Not only that, his stomach was growling furiously. He didn't know how long it had been since he'd had something to eat.

Alex stirred beside him. "What happened?" he asked in a sleepy voice. "Did we get away?"

Ryan shook his head dejectedly.

He could hear footsteps in the tunnel outside. Were the ants coming for them again? Had they devised some new form of torture to get back at the boys for what they had done at the picnic?

An instant later the old ant with the piece missing from its pincer lumbered into the room. It was so huge that it entirely blocked the doorway.

Frightened, Ryan grabbed Alex's hand. His friend was trembling, too.

"If it's going to eat us, I wish it would just get the whole thing over with," Alex sobbed.

Then, as if the monster heard Alex's words, it reared up on its back legs and waved its forelegs wildly in the air. Its pincers slowly began to open.

Ryan let out a howl and threw his arms up over his face to protect himself as the giant pincers opened wider and wider above his head. They were as sharp as knives, and he could almost feel them slash into his flesh.

Alex was clinging to him and whimpering, "It's going to eat us! I told you so!"

Ryan looked frantically for a way out.

Maybe if he punched the bug in the stomach, he could knock the wind out of it. That was what had happened to him once when Raymond punched him in the stomach.

He threw a terrified look back up inside the

insect's jaws. They were open so far now that he could see another set of jaws behind the first set. And behind that were two slimy-looking pockets of flesh.

To Ryan's amazement, the giant bug didn't close its jaws around Ryan's head. Instead, it started dropping objects out of the two pouches, and they landed at Ryan's and Alex's feet.

A dead frog was the first thing to hit the floor. Next came a bunch of seed pods from a maple tree—helicopters, Ryan and his friends always called them. Caterpillars, crickets, and grasshoppers joined the growing pile. Dandelion puffs were next. Then a pair of field mice, dead as doornails, came tumbling out. Finally a blue bird's egg fell out of the ant's mouth and rolled down the side of the growing mound.

The huge ant reached out a front leg and picked up the egg, setting it on top of the pile like a cherry on an ice cream sundae. Then it slowly closed its jaws and pincers and backed out of the room, leaving Ryan and Alex staring after it in stunned silence.

"Look at all this stuff," Alex said in a quivering voice.

"Yeah," Ryan said. "It's like a present or something. But what's it for?"

Suddenly Ryan had a picture of Raymond feeding the ants in the farm on his windowsill. Raymond would go outside and find dead bugs and tiny seeds. He would bring them back to the ant farm and lay the stuff on top of the hill inside the glass box.

The kid would sit for hours watching the ants come up to the top and carry their food down the tunnels. They would store it in some of the little rooms and eventually begin to eat it.

"That's it!" Ryan shouted. "That bugger didn't come in here to eat us! It came to feed us!"

"But why?" Alex demanded. "Those stupid bugs have been trying to kill us. Why would they start feeding us now?"

"I don't know," Ryan admitted. "Do you have a better explanation?"

Alex shook his head and looked at the pile of stuff in front of them. Then he wrinkled his nose. "Yuck! We're supposed to eat *this?*"

Ryan looked back at the dead frogs and mice and bugs. He picked up the blue bird's egg and stirred the seed pods around with a finger.

"Gross," he muttered. Still, he knew those were the kinds of things the ants ate. "What'd you expect, a T-bone steak?" he asked sarcastically.

Alex gave him a nasty look. "Eat it if you want to, but you can count me out. I'd rather starve."

Ryan knew he'd never be hungry enough to eat it, either. Not if he lived inside that anthill for a million years. Not even if the ants barbecued the frog, the mice, and the bugs and served them on a china plate with french fries on the side.

# Chapter

**R**yan and Alex were afraid the ant food would start to stink, so they dug a hole in the soft earth at the back of the cavelike room. They buried all the dead creatures and the bird's egg.

Ryan separated the seed pods and dandelion puffs and left them in the corner. The idea of eating them grossed him out, but he knew there might come a time when they would really need to eat.

Alex peered out into the tunnel. "The coast is clear," he said in a hoarse whisper. "If we're gonna make a break for it, we'd better do it now."

Ryan stepped out into the tunnel and looked in both directions in alarm. "Which way do we go?"

"I dunno," Alex said. He was swiveling his head back and forth, too.

Ryan dropped to his knees and felt the earth. In the shadowy darkness it was hard to see any difference in the slant of the tunnel's floor. But by feeling he could tell that it was slightly higher in one direction and lower in the other.

"Let's go this way," he said, pointing to the left. "The entrance has to be above us, so we might as well walk uphill."

"Good thinking," Alex said.

The boys flattened themselves against the wall of the tunnel and cautiously started moving upward, listening for the slightest sound.

"If you hear any ants coming, duck into the first room you come to," Ryan whispered.

Alex nodded and kept on going forward.

Ryan could hear the faint sounds of insects moving around in some of the connecting tunnels, but so far their luck was holding. The tunnel they were in was empty as far as he could see in either direction.

A moment later they came to a doorway, which turned out to be the entrance to a room.

Ryan glanced in quickly and then stopped and grabbed Alex's belt, making him stop, too. It was dark inside the room, but Ryan could make out a mound of white egg-shaped objects at the far end.

"Larvae!" he whispered to Alex.

"You mean ant eggs?" Alex whispered back.

Ryan nodded. He knew they must be looking at a sort of nursery for ants. He remembered how excited Raymond had gotten when there were larvae in his ant farm.

As his eyes adjusted to the dark room, Ryan could see the eggs more clearly. He froze. A giant ant was huddled over one of the eggs, and he seemed to be slowly and methodically licking it.

Raymond loved watching the worker ants feed and lick the larvae clean until they grew up and hatched.

"Let's get out of here before it figures out we're here," Alex whispered.

But he was too late. Two ants suddenly appeared behind them in the tunnel. A long front leg flicked out and grabbed Alex's arm before the boys could jump out of the way.

Alex struggled and squirmed, but he was powerless beside the ant.

Ryan gasped and stood helplessly watching the giant bug run its antennae over Alex, still holding fast to his arm.

"Ryan! Do something!" Alex screamed. His arms flailed in the air as he tried to break the huge insect's hold on him.

Taking a deep breath, Ryan lunged toward the ant. He grabbed its leg, trying to tear it away from Alex, but it was coiled around his friend like a steel whip.

Ryan felt something tighten around his own arm. The other bug was grasping him with its front leg. Ryan looked around desperately for something to grab on to that would give him the leverage to pull free. But the walls were smooth earth, and there was no way to escape. He kicked at the ant as hard as he could, but that didn't do any good, either.

Ryan cringed, and a cold lump settled in his stomach as the antennae of the insect brushed over him.

*I'm Ryan Miller! A boy!* he wanted to scream. *You can't keep me a prisoner! Let me go!*

Beside him, Alex had covered his face and was whimpering softly.

Ryan held his breath and waited. The giant ant lifted him over its head and marched out into the dark tunnel.

# Chapter

own, down, down they went, deeper into the dank, musty darkness. Ryan grimaced at the sour smell, which was getting stronger and stronger. It reminded him of a can of fishing worms he'd opened once. The worms had been writhing and tumbling all over each other in the slimy, oozy dirt. He'd almost thrown up then, and he felt the same way now.

Ryan rubbed his eyes, trying to force them to see what was up ahead. But the smothering blackness was wrapped around him like a heavy fog.

The sounds of the ant colony grew fainter the farther they traveled downward. Were they heading for some kind of subterranean dungeon? Ryan wondered, shuddering.

Suddenly the two ants halted. Ryan felt the bug's grip loosen, and the next thing he knew, he was tumbling to the ground.

"Ouch," Alex cried as Ryan sprawled on top of him. "Get your foot out of my face!"

"Sorry," Ryan mumbled. He groped around in the darkness until he found a vacant spot on the dirt floor and scrambled to it.

He had no idea if the two ants had stayed with them or had gone back up the tunnel. It was so dark he couldn't see a thing.

"Ryan, where are you?" Alex asked in a trembling voice. "You haven't left me, have you?" It sounded as if he was ready to cry.

"Right here," Ryan replied reassuringly. He felt around in the dark until he found Alex's arm.

"I'm scared. I can't see a thing. I don't know what's happening," Alex sobbed. "I've got to get out of here!"

"I know. Me too," Ryan said. He made his voice sound as calm as he could, but his insides were shaking. And Alex sounded as if he was about to freak.

Ryan opened his eyes wide, hoping his pupils would still be able to adjust to the darkness. Gradually shadows began to form.

"I think they've gone," he said. "At least I can't see them."

"I can't see anything! I don't even know where we are!" Alex cried. "Don't leave me. Okay, Ryan?"

"You know I wouldn't leave you, any more than you'd leave me," Ryan said. He turned over onto his knees, feeling his way around and crawling on his hands and knees.

"Hey, Alex. We're in another room," Ryan said a moment later. "It's awfully small, though, and— What's this?"

He stopped as his hand brushed against a pile of dirt a couple of feet high. Ryan moved his hand a little to one side of it and found a second pile. "This is weird. I wonder what they're for."

"What are *what* for?" Alex asked.

Before Ryan could guess what the dirt piles meant, his ears pricked up. He had heard something again. Something was moving in the tunnel, and it was coming closer. An instant later the shadowy form of an enormous ant filled the doorway.

He heard Alex suck in his breath. He had seen it, too.

The ant came into the room, stopping directly in front of Ryan. It waved its giant antennae as if it was signaling him to do something.

Puzzled, Ryan asked, "Can you figure out what it wants?"

Alex shook his head and scooted farther back into the shadows. The ant stood still for a moment, its feelers quiet, as if it was waiting for something to happen. Its face was turned toward Ryan.

Ryan swallowed hard, trying to think. Did it expect him to do something?

This time when the ant began waving its antennae, it stood up as tall as it could in the low cavelike room and motioned with its forelegs at the same time. It pressed its face close to Ryan's, menacingly moving its pincers from side to side.

"Look out, Ryan! It's going to eat you!" Alex cried.

Ryan backed up as far as he could, pressing

his back against the damp earth and looking up into the monster's face in terror.

The huge insect picked Ryan up and hurled him toward the opposite wall, facefirst. He hit with a *wham!* Pain exploded in his nose.

Ryan slumped back on his haunches and shook his head, spitting out a mouthful of dirt.

The ant loomed over him again. Its pincers were rhythmically opening and closing, opening and closing. Fear gripped Ryan's heart like a clamp. What was the monster going to do next?

He looked frantically around for a way out.

"I'm dead meat if I don't figure out what it wants—and do it right now!"

*Maybe if I try sign language,* he thought desperately. Leaping to his feet, Ryan began gesturing wildly.

The ant stopped and looked at him for a moment, then turned to Alex, dragging him to his feet and shoving him toward the wall.

"No! Leave him alone," Ryan cried frantically. "You've got me. Just show me what you want me to do, okay? I'll do it!"

He knew the ant couldn't understand him. It was useless. It was going to ram him into the wall until it broke his skull, *and there wasn't a thing he could do about it!*

The giant ant reached out and shoved him to his knees next to Alex. If only he could figure out what it wanted!

Finally the big bug lowered itself to the ground beside Ryan and Alex. Using its pincers like a steam shovel, it bit a hunk of dirt out of the wall and added it to one of the piles. Then it bit another hunk of dirt out, and another, adding each one to the mound that was growing taller and taller beside it.

Suddenly Ryan understood. He'd seen Raymond's tiny ants do that very same thing dozens of times. They had used their pincers to dig the dirt out and make the tunnels longer and deeper. Then they had carried the dirt, one grain at a time, out of their nest and up to the surface.

That must be what he and Alex were supposed to do, Ryan realized. Was it possible that when the ants had discovered they couldn't kill him and Alex, they'd decided to turn them into slaves?

# Chapter

**11**

"**C**ome on, Alex. Start digging," Ryan muttered. "That's what it's been trying to tell us."

Alex gave him a puzzled look. "Dig? Are you crazy?"

Ryan glanced around at the ant. It was fidgeting, as if it was starting to get agitated again.

"Just do it," Ryan ordered. "I'll explain in a minute."

He began pawing at the soft earth with his hands, scooping out double handfuls and adding them to the pile closest to him.

Alex watched him for a moment, then heaved a big sigh and started digging, too.

"I *hate* this," Alex grumbled. Tears were running down his face. "I'm hungry, and I want to go home. They can't keep us here. It's against the law!"

"Tell that to them," Ryan retorted, digging harder. "The way I figure it, we're their slaves, and right now there isn't a whole lot we can do about it." His stomach let out a big rumble. "Man, I wish I'd eaten some of the food the ant brought us in that other room."

"Gross!" Alex said. "I'd starve to death before I'd eat a dead frog."

"Not the dead stuff," Ryan said. "Maybe a few helicopters. Just enough to keep my strength up."

"We gotta get out of here!" Alex insisted.

"Fat chance, at least as long as Jaws here is guarding us." He nodded toward the ant, which had settled down with its long body stretched across the room's opening.

"You'd better not call it names," Alex said. "It might understand what you're saying."

"I don't think so," Ryan answered. "And do you know what else? I don't think it can actually see us, either."

Alex stopped digging and looked at Ryan. "Then what are those big eyes for?"

"I don't know, but did you notice how the ants always rub us with their antennae? I think that's how they find us," Ryan said.

"Then if they can't actually see us, we might be able to sneak around them and get away," Alex said, suddenly excited.

"Exactly. As long as we're quiet," Ryan agreed. "The important thing now is to keep digging until we see our chance. Then we'll make a run for it and get out of here before Jaws and its friends can figure out what's happening."

"Okay!" Alex said, a look of relief on his face.

Ryan heard a shuffling sound behind him. Startled, he turned to look at the big ant. It had shifted its position slightly, and now its head rested on the floor.

He nudged Alex. "I think it's asleep," he whispered.

"Lazy bum," Alex muttered. "It should be doing its own digging instead of taking a nap and leaving the work to us slaves."

Ryan moved a little closer to the sleeping ant,

studying it carefully. It was the old guy, the one with the V-shaped piece chipped out of its pincer.

Just then Jaws moved again, and this time it tucked its back end in slightly toward its body, creating a narrow space between itself and the doorway.

Ryan's heart leaped. The gap looked wide enough for Alex and him to slip through.

The space was less than a foot wide, he speculated. Closer to six inches, maybe. If they stepped carefully, they just might make it out without touching the sleeping ant and waking it up, Ryan decided. They had to take the chance.

He tapped Alex on the shoulder and put his finger to his lips to signal silence. Then he pointed to the space between the ant and the doorway.

Alex's eyes opened wide with excitement, and he looked as if he was about to leap for it.

Ryan grabbed his shoulder and gestured for him to settle down. "Don't blow it!" he whispered angrily. "We may not get another chance."

Slowly Ryan got to his feet. Alex did, too.

Holding his breath, Ryan raised his left foot and stepped forward slowly. He stopped, freezing like a statue, and looked at Jaws. The ant hadn't stirred. Then Ryan picked up the other foot and took another slow step, stopping again to check Jaws. When the ant didn't move, he nodded over his shoulder for Alex to follow.

Alex suddenly looked too scared to move. He was staring at Jaws with a terrified expression on his face. Ryan thought he was trembling again.

"I-I can't d-d-do it," Alex stuttered. His mouth was quivering, and he looked as if he was about to cry.

"Yes, you can. Come on," Ryan whispered. He was afraid to say any more, so he pointed straight up and grinned broadly. He hoped Alex would get the message and figure out that he was thinking about the anthill's entrance far over their heads.

Alex hesitated an instant longer and then tiptoed forward. With hand signals, Ryan indicated that he would go through the opening first. Then, being as careful as he could, he began his slow-motion march again. Right foot. Left foot. Right foot. Left foot.

He slipped past the huge, sleeping creature and then cautiously peered out into the tunnel.

# Chapter

**R**yan looked slowly to the right. The coast was clear. He glanced to the left and sucked in his breath in surprise. The tunnel ended just a few feet past the small room he and Alex had been digging out!

He blinked and stared again at the wall of earth where he had expected to see more tunnel. That could only mean that they were in the very deepest part of the anthill, the part of the ant city that was farthest away from the entrance and from freedom.

*Don't panic,* he told himself sternly.

Ryan took another look up the tunnel. Even in the shadowy darkness he could see that nothing was moving and no monstrous insect was lying in wait. The tunnel was deathly still. He and Alex were completely alone in their musty tomb.

"Come on! It's okay!" he whispered over his shoulder to Alex.

His whole body shaking, Alex slipped by the sleeping ant and into the tunnel.

"Stay behind me and keep low to the ground," Ryan instructed. "If we meet an ant, plaster yourself to the wall and be as still as you can. Don't make a sound. If it doesn't touch us, it probably won't know we're there."

Alex nodded to show that he understood, and the boys set out, creeping cautiously up the gentle incline.

After a couple of minutes, Ryan started to breathe easier. This deepest part of the colony didn't seem to be inhabited yet. If they could get high enough before they ran into any ants, they just might be able to make their getaway.

A moment later Ryan's spirits plummeted when he came to a crossroads in the tunnel. Suddenly the tunnels went off in four different directions!

"Which way should we go?" Alex asked.

"I don't know," Ryan said. All the paths probably went up toward the top. But then again, maybe some of them only led to other parts of the subterranean city. Parts where hundreds of ants were busily working.

Ryan stepped over to the tunnel leading off to the right and listened hard for the rustling, scurrying sounds of ants on the move. He couldn't hear anything. He listened at each of the other tunnels. All of them were silent, too.

He sighed. "We'll just have to pick one and take our chances. Come on, let's try this one."

He pointed to the tunnel second from the right. It seemed the steepest. Maybe it was the fastest way to the top. But they hadn't gone very far when he realized he'd made a bad choice.

"Listen," he whispered to Alex. "Do you hear that?"

Alex shook his head as Ryan strained to catch the sound again. It was a sound that was becoming all too familiar. It was the rustling of ants scurrying through tunnels, but there was another sound also, a heavier sound that Ryan had never been aware of before.

And it was coming closer.

"Now I hear it!" Alex cried in alarm.

"We'd better hide!" Ryan said. He looked back down the tunnel. The sound was getting louder fast. It would take too long to run back to the crossroads and duck into a different tunnel. They had to find another place to hide.

"There's a room," Alex said, pointing up the passageway toward an opening.

Ryan didn't take time to answer. He dashed toward the doorway and slipped inside. Alex was right behind him.

It took a minute for Ryan to notice that they were in another nursery. Pale gray ant eggs, the same shape as footballs, only bigger, were piled higher than his head in the center of the room. But in this nursery, there weren't any ants cleaning and tending to the babies.

Outside in the tunnel the sound was getting louder. It sounded as if something heavy was rumbling along in the dirt. It couldn't be very far away now.

Ryan's breath came in short pants as he pressed against the wall of the room and listened. Alex clutched his arm tightly.

"What is it?" he whispered.

Every nerve in Ryan's body was on alert. Whatever was making the noise would pass by the entrance to their hiding place at any second.

"Quick! Hide behind the eggs," he whispered, scrambling across the room and ducking behind the mountain of ant eggs.

Ryan crouched low and listened. In spite of himself, he was shaking. Suddenly the noise stopped—right outside the nursery!

Ryan held his breath and raised his head slowly until he could just see over the edge of the mound. What he saw amazed him. Three giant ants were standing upright in the tunnel just outside the nursery.

Each one of them was balancing at least half a dozen eggs above its head with its front legs. With its middle pair of legs it carried another three or four eggs. And it was pushing another couple of eggs along the tunnel with its back feet. That was what had made the strange rumbling sound. They were bringing another load of eggs into the nursery where he and Alex were hiding!

Ryan suddenly saw something else that made his heart stop.

Alex had not followed him to the hiding place after all. He was flattened against the wall beside the entrance, eyes wide, mouth open, paralyzed with fear.

# Chapter

13

lex looked at Ryan with pleading eyes. His mouth formed a silent "Help!"

Ryan let out an exasperated breath. He couldn't understand why Alex hadn't come with him. So what if he was scared? Ryan was scared, too!

The ants were still outside the door, touching their antennae together and waving them around like crazy. Ryan knew he had to get Alex behind the larvae pile before the ants decided to enter the room.

Alex was still staring at him, but his eyes had the glassy look of someone lost in pure panic. Ryan raised both arms over his head and waved to Alex to move.

Alex didn't even blink, much less run for cover.

"Pssst! Alex! Get over here!" Ryan whispered hoarsely, praying that the ants wouldn't hear him.

Alex still didn't move.

With one eye on the ants outside in the tunnel and the other on Alex, he made a mad dash around the egg pile, grabbed Alex's arm, and yanked him to safety.

"Thanks," Alex murmured. He was breathing hard as they huddled behind the wall of larvae.

At that same instant Ryan heard an ant push an egg across the soft dirt and into the room. Soon all three giant ants were pushing eggs into the small room. Ryan held his breath and listened. They seemed to be rolling the eggs around. Did they have to arrange them a certain way? Were they into interior decorating, too?

Suddenly something zipped into Ryan's range of vision. He watched in horror as one of the football-shaped eggs came wheeling dizzily around the larvae pile and bumped to a stop against his leg. He could feel the dampness on his skin.

Ryan crouched low, his heart racing with fear, and tried to curl up into a ball the size and shape of one of the eggs. Beside him, Alex followed his lead and did the same.

Ryan could hear one of the ants scurrying around the room, looking for the egg that had rolled away. He closed his eyes tightly and burrowed into the mass of warm, pulsing larvae, hoping the ant wouldn't discover him. He shuddered as he thought about the tiny creature forming in each of the eggs he rested against. Each one of them would hatch someday soon and grow into a creature just like Jaws! Then there would be even more ants to keep him and Alex captive.

Suddenly he heard a scratching overhead. Opening one eye, he peeked up. A giant ant was sweeping its antennae over the mound of eggs. It was searching for the stray egg, and its antennae were coming closer and closer to him.

The next instant it brushed his back. Ryan cringed in fear as it hesitated a minute and then rubbed back and forth as if it was trying to figure out what had sneaked into the egg pile.

He tried to burrow in deeper, but by now the

ant had a firm grip on him. He felt himself being pulled into the middle of the room by a huge insect using its front legs like giant tweezers.

Another ant had found Alex.

"Ryan! Help me!" Alex cried as he was lifted high over the head of his captor.

"I can't help you!" Ryan yelled back in exasperation. "One of them has me, too!"

The ant set Ryan down on the floor and pushed him toward the egg pile. Then it pulled out an egg and began gently rubbing and licking it.

Alex had been set down beside Ryan, and his eyes were wide with disbelief.

"They—they don't—" Alex began.

"They want us to clean the eggs," Ryan guessed suddenly. Jaws had shown them by example that he wanted the room dug out. Now this ant was showing them how to take care of the eggs in the nursery.

"I'm not going to lick any ant eggs!" Alex burst out. He jumped to his feet, but the ant standing behind him quickly pushed him to his knees again.

Ryan thought quickly. "Maybe we could just wipe them off with our hands," he suggested.

"You mean, like, *dust* them?" Alex asked in amazement.

"It's worth a try," Ryan said.

Alex shook his head.

Ryan reached for an egg near the top of the pile and rolled it slowly onto the floor in front of him. Then, darting a fearful glance at the ant looming over him, he slowly wiped his hand over the surface of the egg.

It was all he could do to touch the lumpy, pulsing thing. The skin of the egg was warm and leathery. He could feel the unborn ant moving around inside.

What if it suddenly hatched? he wondered in alarm. What if it popped out of its egg, all covered with gooey, slimy stuff, and got its slime all over him?

Ryan felt a funny, pulling sensation at the back of his tongue, and his stomach started to roll.

Suddenly the big ant nudged him. Ryan got hold of himself and started wiping the egg like crazy.

"Hurry up," he ordered Alex. "We've got to get all these suckers clean before they start hatching."

But the ant still wasn't happy. It poked Ryan again and began licking the disgusting egg, carefully moistening the shell all over.

Alex took one look and started to freak.

"I told you I'm not going to lick an ant egg!" he yelled at the top of his lungs. "They can kill me first. I won't do it!" Then he scrambled toward the doorway on all fours.

All three ants reared up on their back legs and waved their antennae in his direction.

Ryan knew that they would lunge for him any second.

"Alex!" he screamed. "I've got an idea! You won't have to lick them! Not really! I promise!"

Alex stopped and looked back over his shoulder at Ryan. At the same instant his expression changed to terror as he caught sight of the three giant ants poised to pounce.

"Come on, Alex!" Ryan shouted again. "Do it!"

It was as if a switch had flipped in Alex's brain. He instantly dropped flat on the floor, dodging the ants' attack, and slithered back to Ryan.

"This had better be good," he muttered.

"See, this is all you have to do," Ryan said. He gathered all the saliva he could in his mouth and spit it onto the egg. Then he took his hand and rubbed the liquid all over the surface.

The three ants hovered above them, touching Ryan and then the egg. Ryan spit again and made sure there wasn't a single spot anywhere on the egg that wasn't wet.

Alex had been watching Ryan's every move in disgust, but he grabbed an egg off the pile and spit on it, looking up warily at the three ants as he spread the saliva all over it.

They rubbed their feelers over him and the egg. Then two of them stationed themselves beside the door, while the third one disappeared into the tunnel.

"Looks like they're happy, but they're also going to make sure we don't try to sneak out," Ryan whispered, spitting on a second egg. "At least they won't hurt us as long as we keep cleaning eggs."

"But what if we run out of spit?" Alex insisted.

Ryan didn't answer. He'd been thinking the same thing, and already his mouth was starting to feel dry.

# Chapter

14

The longer Ryan crouched on the floor cleaning the ant eggs with his spit, the drier his mouth got. He could barely swallow, and his tongue felt like a big slab of cardboard. He sucked and sucked to try to pull more saliva into his mouth, but his entire body felt as if it was going completely dry.

He was starting to think about other problems, too. He had no idea how long he and Alex had been in their subterranean prison. It could have been hours or even a couple of days, for all he knew. They hadn't had anything to eat or drink. He was terribly hungry, and his head was nodding and his eyelids drooping as he got more and more desperate for sleep. *But I don't want to go to sleep!* he thought angrily, snapping to attention. *I want to go home!*

"Alex," he whispered anxiously, "we've got to *do* something! We can't stay down here forever."

"You're telling me! But what?" Alex grumbled, wiping an egg he had just pulled off the pile. "Those stupid ants are guarding the door. They're never going to let us get past them."

"Maybe there's a way," Ryan said thoughtfully. He was looking up at the tall mound of eggs. "Maybe we could create a distraction."

"Like what?" Alex asked skeptically.

"Like an egg avalanche," Ryan said excitedly.

"A *what?*" asked Alex, making a face.

"You heard me. An egg avalanche. If we could get all these suckers moving at once, those ants would be so busy trying to round them up that we could make a break for it." Ryan felt his excitement growing. "I think it would work."

"Yeah, maybe," Alex said. He hesitated. "But even if we got out into the tunnel, we'd still be in trouble." He rubbed one of the bruises on his arm, and Ryan instinctively touched the tender welt on his side.

"It's the only chance we've got, unless you can come up with something better," Ryan assured him. "We're not going to get out of this anthill by cleaning stinky eggs all day."

Alex didn't say anything for a moment. Ryan knew he was thinking it over. Finally he sighed and said, "Okay. How do we start this avalanche, anyway?"

"Just do what I do," Ryan said.

He began slowly moving around the side of the egg pile, pretending to be cleaning the eggs. He kept an eye on the ants that were guarding the door.

Alex scooted along beside him.

"Okay, here goes," Ryan whispered when they were on the back side of the mound of eggs. Taking a giant leap, he scrambled halfway up the side of the egg pile and reached a hand down to pull Alex up with him.

At first he could feel the tiny bodies squirming and wiggling around inside the eggs. He pushed and shoved the eggs with his feet, and the whole pile started trembling. Some of the eggs started to roll off the pile. Above him, the eggs on the top were bouncing up and down. He teetered and swayed, throwing his weight against the mound of larvae, trying to get them to topple down.

"Come on, Alex! This thing's going to go any second!" he yelled, fighting to keep his balance as the movement grew.

An instant later, Alex was beside him. "Whoa!" Alex shouted as the mountain of eggs heaved and shuddered like a volcano about to blow.

Ryan put both of his hands against the wall of eggs and motioned for Alex to do the same.

"Now shove as hard as you can and jump free," he instructed. "Then as soon as the ants leave the door, make a run for it."

Alex nodded sharply and put out his hands.

"On the count of three," Ryan muttered. "One . . . two . . . *three!* Shove!"

Ryan heaved himself against the mound and felt it tottering. The eggs beneath his feet gave way. He pitched forward into a blizzard of whitish-gray larvae that swirled around in every direction. Suddenly, to his horror, an egg slammed into the side of his head and burst open, sloshing putrid goo all over his face and arms.

Spitting and gagging, Ryan wiped away the goo as best he could. He was still tumbling through the mass of eggs, and he couldn't see Alex anywhere.

"Alex!" he cried. "Are you okay?"

Alex didn't answer. But before Ryan could call out again, he slammed to the ground, crushing two more ant eggs with his knees.

"Eewwwwwww," he groaned as he held his breath and tried to wipe off his pants.

The eggs were pelting the floor like snowballs. In the midst of the storm, the two ants scrambled to stop the larvae from rolling out the door.

Then Ryan saw Alex crouching in a corner, trembling. He raced to him, and together they plastered themselves against the wall near the door and waited. By now the third ant had come back into the room and was helping the other two gather the eggs and push them toward the back of the room. But eggs were still rolling around on the floor and falling from the pile.

Ryan held his breath. One of the ants passed dangerously close, but its feelers were tapping the ground in front of it like a pair of blind men's canes.

Ryan glanced nervously at Alex. He wanted to make a break for it right away, but he was filled with terror. Maybe Alex was right. Maybe they'd only get out into the tunnel and then get captured again—bitten and stung, and carried even deeper into the darkness to stay buried alive forever.

*No!* he thought frantically.

"Now!" he shouted. He grabbed Alex by the arm, and the two of them went careening out into the shadowy tunnel.

# Chapter

15

The boys ran up the sloping tunnel as fast as they could go, trying to put as much distance as possible between themselves and their captors.

So far, at least, they were alone in the passageway, but Ryan knew that Jaws or some other ant could come charging after them any second. Each time they saw a doorway they stopped and approached it cautiously, holding their breath and listening before they dared peer inside.

Finally, exhausted, Alex slowed down and slumped against the wall. His chest was heaving. "I don't think I can go any farther," he said, shaking his head wearily. "I'm beat."

"But we can't stop now," Ryan insisted. He tugged at Alex's arm, but Alex wouldn't budge.

"I've got to have something to eat," Alex said. "And I'm thirsty. I couldn't spit any more if I had to."

"I know how you feel," Ryan admitted. His stomach had been growling unmercifully. "I could eat a horse and drink gallons of water, but we've got to keep going while the coast is clear."

Alex gave him a dirty look and pushed off from the wall with a foot. He trudged up the incline beside Ryan without saying a word.

Suddenly Ryan thought he heard a sound somewhere ahead of them. He stopped and pricked up his ears. It was the sound of marching ants. Fifty or a hundred of them, maybe.

"We've gotta hide!" he whispered quickly.

But there wasn't time. The ants were in sight now, rounding a bend. A whole column, standing upright on their back legs and carrying enormous bundles of leaves and grass over their heads. They were marching straight toward the boys with military precision.

Ryan looked around wildly, but there was no place to hide.

"Don't forget, they probably can't see us," he reminded Alex. "If we stay quiet, the only way they'll know we're here is if they accidentally feel us with their antennae."

"So?" grumbled Alex. "How are they going to miss touching us? They're taking up practically the whole tunnel."

Ryan couldn't answer his friend. He pressed himself against the wall and watched the ants march closer and closer. He sucked in his gut, holding his breath until he thought he would explode. One bumped him with its hind part, but it was so intent on what it was doing, it didn't notice him.

Ten . . . twenty . . . thirty ants. Ryan lost count, and he closed his eyes. It didn't matter how many there were. The important thing was, they didn't know he and Alex were there. He opened his eyes again and saw that the last one had passed.

"I wonder what that stuff they were carrying was and where they were taking it," Alex said once the tunnel was quiet again.

Ryan started to shrug, but a thought occurred to him.

"I'll bet that was food," he said excitedly. "I know that worker ants leave the anthill to gather food that they bring back to the colony. I've seen Raymond's ants do that, too. And then they store it in little rooms where other ants go when they get hungry."

"So you think they're dumping that stuff into a room somewhere farther down the tunnel, near where we just came from?" asked Alex.

"It makes sense," Ryan replied. "There would be plenty of space. A bunch of those rooms were empty. If we can just find where they stored it, maybe we can get something to eat that'll keep us going until we get out of here."

"Yeah, I'm almost hungry enough to eat dead stuff," Alex muttered.

"We won't have to eat dead stuff," Ryan assured him. "They were carrying leaves and things. I could eat a leaf any day of the week." He paused and held up his hand for quiet. "Uh-oh. I hear them again. They're coming back this way."

The boys backed up to the wall again and held

their breath as the scurrying ants began passing them and heading back toward the top of the hill. The bugs were moving more slowly now and less like a military formation. There were gaps in their ranks, and a couple of times a pair of ants stopped within inches of Ryan and Alex to carry on conversations with their antennae.

Ryan spotted a straggler making its way up the tunnel. That was the direction he and Alex needed to go if they were going to search for the room where the food was stashed.

But the ant seemed to be in no hurry. It sauntered along as if it had all week.

*Hurry up, you stupid bug!* Ryan wanted to yell.

Alex had spotted it, too, and was frowning at it intently. Then Alex's expression changed to fear.

Ryan threw a fast glance at the ant again and did a double take. A V-shaped chip was missing from the pincer on its left side.

It was Jaws!

Both boys gasped and shrank back farther, watching Jaws as it crept along on all six legs, sweeping its antennae from one side of the tunnel to the other as if it was looking for something. Its viselike pincers swung back and forth in front of its face. Any second it would be within feeling range of the boys.

Ryan knew instantly what Jaws was looking for. *Them!*

He backed against the wall in terror, and as he did, his hand touched something hard in the surface of the dirt. He dug at it with his fingers. A rock about the size of the palm of his hand came loose, and he gripped it hard. Could he fight off the beast with it?

He looked at the six powerful legs and the razor-sharp pincers and knew he didn't have a chance. He had to think of something else—fast!

Alex clutched at Ryan's arm. "Does it know we're here?" he whispered.

Ryan shook his head and frowned at Alex. He put a finger against his lips to signal for quiet. There was no point in helping Jaws by making noise and giving themselves away.

Ryan bounced the rock in his hand as he tried to think. His brain had turned to mush, and Jaws had almost reached them.

Suddenly the weight and shape of the rock in his hand jolted him to his senses. It might just save them after all.

# Chapter

yan looked at Jaws again and shuddered. The enormous ant was lumbering up the incline on all sixes, using its antennae like land-mine detectors. There was no way it could miss the boys if it kept coming.

The rock was flat, just right for skipping across a pond. But this wasn't a pond. It was a dark anthill, deep underground. Ryan took a long, slow breath and stepped out into the center of the tunnel like a pitcher stepping onto the mound. Jaws was only a few feet behind him now. Ryan knew he would have only one chance, so he had to do it right.

He crouched low. Scanning the tunnel to get

his bearings, he turned slightly, then hurled the rock sidearmed up the incline. He held his breath as he heard it hit the floor and bounce, skipping three more times before it came to rest.

Suddenly Jaws reared up on its hind legs, waving its forelegs in the air and pointing its antennae like a pair of arrows toward the sound of the skipping rock.

Ryan flattened himself against the wall again, just in time to see the giant ant race by.

He was flooded with relief. "Jaws heard it!" he whispered to Alex excitedly. "It thinks that we're up ahead!"

Ryan dashed up the tunnel after the huge creature. After a few dozen feet he dropped to his knees and frantically felt around in the dirt for the rock. Nothing. The floor was smooth and damp. He crawled a little farther, sweeping his hands back and forth across the floor. It had to be there somewhere. He knew Jaws hadn't stopped to pick it up.

As he was groping through the dirt his hand suddenly touched something hard. It was the rock, wedged into the soft earth where the floor met the wall. Breathing a sigh of relief, he put it in his pocket. It might come in handy again.

Ryan rejoined Alex, and the boys crept slowly down the incline. If they didn't find food soon, they wouldn't have enough strength to escape.

Ryan took the lead again as they inched their way along. His skin prickled with fear. His ears strained for the slightest sound.

The first room they came to was empty. Scattered remnants of broken eggshells told Ryan that it had recently been a nursery.

They passed two more rooms that were totally empty. But then, cautiously peeking into the third room, Ryan saw exactly what they'd been looking for.

"All right," Alex said, grinning from ear to ear at the sight of mounds and mounds of leaves, grasses, and seed pods. "It's feast time!"

Ryan dropped to his knees and stuffed handfuls of grass and leaves into his mouth. It tasted delicious! He ground the leaves between his teeth and sucked out the moisture. He wolfed the seed pods down whole, stopping only when the pods stuck between his teeth.

Next to him, Alex was chewing noisily and

grinning as green juice ran down his chin. "Man, this is great," he said between bites. "I never knew this kind of stuff was so delicious. Next time I'll order this instead of a cheeseburger!"

As Ryan's stomach began to fill up, he started wandering among the mounds of food. To his relief, there wasn't any dead stuff, but there was plenty of greenery. He noticed some branches, and a new idea began to form in his mind. He'd been thinking about it for a long time, but until now he hadn't had the slightest idea how to carry it out.

He found a thick branch with a forked end and stripped off its leaves. Next he searched among the grasses until he found a long weed that was too tough to break.

"What are you doing?" Alex asked.

Ryan didn't answer. He drew the flat rock out of his pocket and positioned it in the fork at the top of the branch. Next he wound the weed around and around both the rock and the branch until the stone was securely fastened.

"A tomahawk!" he said triumphantly. "See? Just like the Indians used to make." He raised it into the air and started dancing around the room, circling in and out around the piles of food.

"Wow!" Alex said. His voice was filled with admiration. "Do you really think we can fight off the ants with that?"

"Probably not," Ryan admitted. "It wouldn't be much of a match for their pincers, especially if a bunch of them came after us at once." Then he smiled slyly and added, "But I've got a better idea. We'll use it to kill the queen."

Alex's eyes became solemn. "The *queen?*" he whispered in disbelief. "How are we going to do that?"

"First we have to find her nest," Ryan said. "In Raymond's ant farm it was near the top of the hill. That's where we're going to look."

"Hey, wait a minute," Alex said, frowning. "If I get to the top, I'm outta here."

"After we kill the queen," Ryan said firmly, "the colony will go crazy. Getting out after that will be easy. They'll be in too much of a panic even to follow us. Don't you see? We've got to destroy the colony once and for all."

"I don't know," Alex said slowly. "It sounds pretty risky to me."

"Of course it's risky," Ryan said. "But it's the only way we're ever going to get out of here. There isn't time to look for another rock, so find yourself a strong stick. We'll use the tomahawk to sharpen it into a spear. *Then* we'll go after the queen."

Reluctantly Alex began digging through the piles of leaves until he found a branch strong enough to be a weapon. He watched soberly as Ryan pounded it into a pointed spear and handed it back to him.

"We'd better take some food along," Ryan said. "We sure can't come back here every time we get hungry."

Both boys filled their pockets with helicopters and other leaves and seeds.

Ryan put his arm around Alex's shoulder. "If this doesn't work, probably nothing will," he said solemnly. "But I think we're ready."

Ryan felt a lump forming in his throat as he looked sadly at the friend he'd known all his life. "We'll always be best buddies, no matter what. Okay?"

"Okay!" Alex answered, trying to smile.

They exchanged high fives and headed for the tunnel.

# Chapter

17

Ryan's heart was in his throat as he and Alex picked their way through the dusky tunnel. As he scanned the walls of the passageway he was amazed at how well his eyes had adjusted to the darkness of the subterranean city. He could see things now that he hadn't been able to make out when he first arrived.

Tree roots snaked up the walls and over the ceilings. Tiny bugs burrowed into the dirt. Even an occasional earthworm pushed through the soil, reaching its eyeless head out to feel its surroundings like a blind man reaching out a hand. It was a whole new world down there, a world Ryan could hardly wait to get out of.

"It sure is quiet," Alex remarked after a while.

Ryan had noticed it, too. He couldn't remember when the ant colony had been so silent.

They followed the turns and twists of the tunnels, sometimes turning left at an intersection, sometimes turning right, always trying to find the path leading most steeply upward toward the entrance to the hill.

The higher they climbed, the more activity they encountered. Ants were scurrying every which way, each one so intent on its job that Ryan and Alex seldom had to dodge their feelers.

As soon as they rounded the next bend, Ryan felt a flash of pain in his eyes. He threw his arm up over his face. Slowly peering up over it, he realized that the tunnel was getting lighter.

"We must be getting close to the top," he whispered over his shoulder to Alex.

They stopped for a moment to get used to the strange new light. Alex was squinting in the brightness, and yet Ryan knew it was still pretty dim compared to the outside world.

Another army of ants rushed by. This time

they were all carrying pincer-loads of dirt out of the caverns below to be deposited at the top of the hill.

Ryan ducked into another cavelike room just before they thundered past. His excitement was growing. But so was his fear. They were in grave danger now. The ant colony had turned into a bustling city.

"We'd better stay on our toes," he whispered to Alex as two more ants passed the doorway balancing eggs on their heads.

That gave Ryan an idea.

He nudged Alex. "Did you see those ants that just went by, carrying eggs?"

Alex nodded.

"They had to be coming from the queen's nesting room," he said excitedly. "At least we know we're heading in the right direction."

"Yeah, but they were coming this way, not going toward it," Alex reminded him. "What good does that do?"

"Just before we ducked in here, I saw an intersection up ahead where three tunnels come together," Ryan said jubilantly. "All I have to do is slip out and watch the intersection. I'll be able to see which tunnel the ants with the eggs come out of. It's a cinch! We'll know exactly which way to go to find the queen!"

# Chapter

**R**yan grabbed his tomahawk and bolted toward the door, pausing to make sure the coast was clear before leaving the safety of the room.

They were getting unbelievably close to escaping now. He felt the excitement bubbling up as he thought about himself and Alex finally climbing out of the anthill and racing home free.

He shrank into the shadows and dropped to all fours, ready to jump at the slightest hint of danger. Squinting in the eerie light, he tried to see in all directions at once so he wouldn't miss anything.

Just then an ant bustled by, brushing the floor

with its forelegs and sweeping a small pile of dirt and twigs in front of it.

*It must be cleaning house,* Ryan thought in amazement.

His attention was drawn to sounds coming from the middle tunnel. It was the low rumbling noise he'd heard before. Ants were rolling eggs to a new nursery!

Ryan clutched his tomahawk and squeezed himself back as far as he could into the shadows as the first of the ants came into view. Like the other insects in this busy part of the colony, they were paying attention only to their work and kept their feelers trained on the eggs so that they wouldn't roll off in the wrong direction.

Ryan held his breath as they went past him. First there were only two. Then a third ant came hurrying down the passageway. A fourth and fifth came along a minute later. Each one carried at least two eggs on its head, one egg clasped at its midsection, and one rolling in front along the ground.

He waited, staring up the middle tunnel and listening. After a few minutes of quiet, he knew it was time to put the next part of his plan into action.

"Alex! Come on!" he cried, sticking his head into the room.

Alex was sitting on the floor, clutching his spear and looking scared again. "I d-d-don't know," he stuttered.

"You can't back out now," Ryan said angrily. "We'll make it! I promise! Just stay behind me and keep low."

Reluctantly Alex got to his feet and followed Ryan. The tunnel was still quiet.

Slowly, one step at a time, they started up the central passageway. The hairs on the back of Ryan's neck stood up, and he could hear his blood pounding in his ears.

Behind him, Alex had a death grip on his arm.

Suddenly Ryan noticed that the passageway seemed different. It was getting steeper, but that wasn't what bothered him. It was something else. Something he couldn't quite put his finger on. Then it hit him. The tunnel was getting narrower! In fact, it was getting so narrow that he wondered in alarm if one ant could walk through without touching the sides!

"Hurry, Alex!" he called over his shoulder.

"This place is tightening up. We've got to get to the queen before any more ants come this way!"

He sprinted forward, hoping Alex was doing the same. He was panting breathlessly, and his legs pumped hard, but the tunnel seemed to be getting steeper and narrower every step of the way.

Just then he heard a sound coming up from behind them.

"Oh, no!" he cried.

The sound of marching ants was coming closer.

Ryan whirled around to face Alex. "We're stopping here," he commanded. He ignored Alex's horrified look and kept on barking orders.

"Use your spear to dig out a hole in the wall—a space big enough for you to fit into. Then smear dirt all over yourself so that if they touch you, they'll think you're part of the wall. Go on," he yelled. "It's our only chance."

Mutely Alex began attacking the base of the wall with his spear. Ryan pulled his tomahawk out of his belt and did the same.

He could hear the ants coming closer.

Ryan dug harder. Faster. Dirt crumbled and fell around his feet. He could hear Alex whimpering as he pounded the wall with his spear. Would they make it in time? Ryan wondered.

*Maybe we should have worked together and dug one big hole,* Ryan thought frantically, but he knew it was too late to change their plan.

He scooped the dirt out with his hands and scrunched inside his niche. Pressing himself firmly into the hole, he pulled the dirt back in around himself. He rubbed the damp, musty dirt all over himself, then lay very still and listened.

The ants were coming.

He held his breath and peered out as the feet of three ants passed by in single file. Their antennae were wrapped around the object they carried over their heads.

He stifled a gasp as he saw what that object was—*the corpse of a dead ant!*

He was watching a funeral procession. The bugs were heading out of the anthill to bury their dead.

Ryan grimaced at the gruesome sight. Would the next corpses the ants carried out be Ryan's and Alex's?

# Chapter

After the procession had passed, Ryan stared gloomily at the dirt floor of the tunnel and thought about his mother and father. And Raymond. Would they miss him? Or would his parents be so proud of his little brother's good grades that they'd forget all about him? Would they think, *Good riddance. Who needs such a dumb kid, anyway?* He couldn't even make good grades. And Raymond would probably get to take over his room and all his important stuff—if he hadn't already!

The idea made Ryan furious. Raymond had better stay out of his room and away from his private property if he knew what was good for him. The nerdy little brat would mess everything up! It wasn't fair!

Ryan's blood was starting to boil. He couldn't let Raymond get away with a thing like that.

He stuck his head out of the hole and whispered hoarsely, *"Pssst,* Alex! Come on, let's kill that queen and get out of here!"

Slowly Alex's head appeared at the top of his hole, and he gave Ryan an owlish look.

"Can't we just . . . get out of here, without killing the queen?"

"I told you, we've got to destroy the colony," Ryan said impatiently. "It's our best chance for escape!"

He gripped his tomahawk and crawled out of the hole. Standing up, he shook off the dirt and started up the hill. He had taken only a few steps when he saw a trickle of water rolling down the center of the tunnel floor.

"Hey, look. It must be raining outside, and the water's coming in through the entrance to the mound," he said.

Alex nodded absently, and Ryan knew he was too scared to care.

They plodded on. The hill was even steeper than before, and the boys began panting.

"I wonder how much longer," Alex whispered.

Ryan shrugged. The stream of water was wider now and running faster. He saw a bend in the tunnel up ahead, and he braced himself for what might be beyond it.

He could hear the hum of activity.

"This could be it," he whispered to Alex. "We can't be scared. We just have to do it." He was talking as if he felt braver than he really was, but he knew his words were true.

Slowly he peeked around the bend—and jumped back immediately.

"It's up there!" he whispered. "I'd bet a million dollars that's where the queen is. There are a couple of big buggers guarding the door to one of the rooms. It's *got* to be her nest!"

Alex nodded solemnly and tightened his grip on his spear. His eyes got even wider with fright.

*It's now or never,* Ryan thought. "Okay, Alex. We're going!"

Staying flat against the wall, Ryan took the first step around the corner. He fastened his eyes on the guards. They hadn't heard him. In fact, they were slumped against the wall—maybe resting, maybe sleeping.

He took another step, careful to slide along without making a sound. Then another. And another. Alex was following, his spear poised in front of him.

They were less than a yard away now. Ryan swallowed hard and tried to slow his breathing. Cold chills ran up and down his spine. He gritted his teeth. He couldn't panic. Not now! They were too close.

Suddenly the antennae on one of the guards started twitching and flicking.

Ryan froze and watched the feelers snake around and search the air. He knew he hadn't made a sound. How could the ant possibly know they were there?

He threw a frantic look down the tunnel. They could still retreat! They could race down the tunnel and hide in a room.

He swallowed hard. No! He couldn't slink away in defeat. Not when they were this close.

He glanced quickly up the tunnel beyond the queen's chamber. Freedom was in that direction.

How far could it be? But even if he and Alex made it, the ants would come after them, swarming all over the countryside, attacking their town, maybe killing their families and friends.

Ryan knew they had to kill the queen and destroy the colony.

The ant was still waving its antennae, only now it was touching the second ant. Ryan watched in horrified fascination as they seemed almost to shake hands with their feelers. He knew they were talking to each other.

"The first one's telling the other one that it senses danger in the tunnel," Ryan whispered to Alex. "We have to make our move now! Geronimo!" he screamed, and dove headlong through the space between the guards. He hit the floor rolling and came to a thudding stop against a huge jellylike blob that quivered when he hit it. He looked up.

It was the queen!

Alex barely made it into the room ahead of the guards, but his eyes were gleaming and his face looked excited as he repeated Ryan's battle cry.

"Geronimo!"

The ants were coming on fast, bumping into each other and tangling their legs and pincers as they struggled to get into the room.

Ryan looked at the bulbous form beside him. She was big and sluggish. Her body was lumpy from all the eggs, and on the floor surrounding her were piles of newly laid larvae.

The guards were through the door now, and Ryan could hear more ants running toward them in the tunnel. The insects' feelers were slicing the air, and their ropelike legs were grabbing for the boys.

Ryan swung his tomahawk over his head. It would take all the strength he had to plunge it into the queen's soft underbelly with enough force to kill her.

The guard ants were advancing, their pincers snapping and their stingers swishing like sharp swords. He knew he had only one chance.

Suddenly the guards froze in midstep. Very slowly they relaxed their legs. Their antennae went limp.

"What's happening?" Alex asked anxiously.

"I dunno," said Ryan. "Unless . . . unless they

can sense that their queen is in danger, and they're backing off."

The thrill of victory raced up Ryan's spine as he watched ants by the dozens gather in the tunnel outside the room. None of them raised a menacing leg. Their pincers were closed. Their antennae barely flickered as they passed the news to one another and shrank back.

Ryan took a deep breath and raised the tomahawk higher. He was going to enjoy this.

A little grin played over Alex's face as he pointed his spear at the queen.

"On the count of three," said Ryan. "One . . . two . . . thr—" He gasped. "No! Stop, Alex! We can't do it!"

Alex pulled back his spear, which was only inches from the queen's fat belly. "Why not?" he demanded.

"Don't you see? The only reason the ants aren't attacking us right now is because they're afraid we're going to hurt their queen."

"You mean, once we go ahead and kill her, they won't have any reason to back off anymore?" Alex asked. Fear had returned to his voice.

"Exactly," Ryan said, looking at the horde of ants facing them. "They'll never let us out of here alive!"

# Chapter

**R**yan felt trapped as he looked at the army of ants lined up against them.

"What are we going to do now?" Alex asked in a quivering voice.

"I wish I knew," Ryan replied. Everything was wrong. They were faced with an army of enemy ants, and there was no place to run. His arms were going numb from holding the tomahawk over his head, but if he put it down, the ants would rush him.

He glanced at the queen out of the corner of his eye. She was just lying there like a mountain of jelly. Her antennae didn't move, and her pincers were closed.

Alex was looking at her, too. "She's not much to look at, is she?" he asked. "Just a big blob. I'll bet she can't even stand up, much less defend herself."

Ryan blinked and looked at her again. "Alex, you're a genius," he said excitedly.

"Why? What did I say?" Alex asked, looking bewildered.

"Maybe we can use her as a hostage!"

"You mean kidnap her?"

"Why not? If she can't fight us off and she can't run away, then maybe we can drag her up the passageway to the exit."

"How are you going to explain that to them?" Alex snorted. "Do you know feeler language?"

"They'll get the idea," Ryan assured him, but deep down he wasn't so sure.

The boys nudged the queen and she moved slightly, as if she was trying to get out of their way.

"I'll pull on her head, and you shove her backside and poke her with your spear," Ryan ordered. "Since we'll be facing each other, we can watch each other's backs."

"Okay," came the muffled reply.

They grabbed on to the queen's slippery body and inched forward, pushing and tugging the big insect toward the nesting room's exit. The throng of guard ants stood motionless.

The closer the boys got, the harder Ryan's heart pounded. What if it didn't work? What if the ants jumped on them anyway? He dug his fingers into the queen's oozy flesh to get a tighter hold.

Mysteriously, the ants parted, opening a path into the tunnel. Maybe the queen did have a way to communicate with them.

Breathless, Ryan pulled the front half of the queen into the passage. "Give her a good shove," he called to Alex.

Alex must have heaved with all his might, because the rest of the big ant popped through the door and into the tunnel, almost knocking Ryan off his feet. It was like trying to move a giant water balloon.

He scrambled to get his balance, splashing into the trickle of water that had now turned into a river. He landed on his back, slipping and sliding all over the place, still clutching the ant queen's head as well as his tomahawk.

He quickly put the hatchet back into his belt and grabbed hold of a tree root to stop his downward slide. At the same time he kept a tight grip on the ant queen.

"Alex! Help!" he cried.

Alex heaved upward with his shoulder and wedged himself under her bulk.

"I can't! She's too heavy!" he cried, his legs losing their grip in the slippery mud.

Ryan looked around frantically. He wasn't sure how long he could hold on to both the root and the ant. Then he spotted a longer root dangling from the ceiling just to his left.

"You've got to!" he shouted back. "Just for a minute!"

Cautiously he let go of the queen's head. She slid down a little way and stopped. Good old Alex was hanging on!

Ryan reached up and grabbed the long root, jerking as hard as he could. Nothing happened. He jerked again, trying desperately to break it off, but the root held. Then he remembered his tomahawk.

He hacked at the root with all his might. It gave way. He looped it quickly around the queen's neck, then wrapped it once again around the upper part of her body to create a harness. Now he could drag her more easily, he thought with relief.

Suddenly he saw Jaws advancing with a crowd of ants. Ryan raised his tomahawk above the queen. Jaws pawed at the air and then backed off.

"It's okay!" Ryan shouted. "I've got her now. Come here and help me! We're almost to the top!"

An instant later, Alex's smiling face bobbed up beside him.

"It's gonna work!" Alex shouted. "We're gonna get free!"

Inch by inch, they fought and struggled their way upward through the gushing water and over the slippery mud.

"Look!" Alex shouted excitedly. He pointed over his head. "I can see it!"

Ryan looked up in awe at a pinpoint of light. It was the opening they'd been dreaming about—the entrance to the anthill.

*No,* he thought. *The exit from the anthill and the entrance to freedom!*

The sight gave him a new burst of energy. He could do anything now!

He kept his eye on the pinpoint of light, watching it grow bigger and bigger as he and Alex dug in their heels and dragged the huge ant steadily toward it.

Suddenly a dark form blotted out the light.

The next instant something came crashing down, landing squarely on top of Ryan and Alex.

To Ryan's horror, he felt the heavy queen slip out of his hands and slide swiftly away into the dark abyss below.

Chapter 21

"**R**aymond!" Ryan shouted an instant later.

His little brother grinned, showing the spaces where his two front teeth should have been.

"I knew you'd be—" Raymond stopped short and terror filled his eyes as he looked downward.

The tunnel was in chaos as dozens of monster ants swarmed around the queen, pushing and shoving each other, trying to get close to her. Others lined up beneath her, trying in unison to heave her back toward her nesting room.

"They're—they're—they're so huge," Raymond gasped.

"They're giants. We'll explain later. Let's get out of here!" Ryan cried. He tried desperately to scramble up the last few feet of tunnel to the opening, but he slipped and slid backward into the mud. He could see streaks of rain coming down outside. Water poured in from the entrance and sloshed around him, making progress impossible.

"What are we gonna do?" Alex shouted. He was on his stomach, covered with mud. His arms and legs were flailing furiously as he tried in vain to climb the tunnel.

Ryan couldn't answer. He needed all his strength to struggle upward. Suddenly he remembered Raymond. Where had the little kid gone? Looking over his shoulder, he saw his brother clinging to a root and kicking furiously at the huge ant looming over him.

Ryan did a double take. The ant had a V-shaped chip missing from its pincer. It was Jaws!

Jaws wrapped a steely leg around Raymond's waist and jerked him so hard that Raymond lost his grip on the root.

"Help!" he screamed at the top of his lungs. "Ryan! Help me!"

The big ant lifted Raymond over its head and waved its antennae wildly. It carried the screaming boy like a trophy as it slowly descended past Ryan and Alex and into the darkness.

Ryan's heart stopped. He couldn't let Jaws take his little brother! Using the tunnel like a water slide, Ryan dove headfirst toward Jaws. Water filled his nose and splashed over him. It stung his eyes. He blinked hard, trying to keep the big ant in view.

Suddenly Jaws stopped, letting the water swirl around its legs. It turned the top of its body around and opened his pincers.

Ryan realized in a flash what was happening, and he tried to stop. But the rushing water was carrying him toward Jaws at terrific speed. He tried to roll toward drier ground, grab a root— anything. But the water kept carrying him forward. He crashed to a stop against Jaws's huge stomach.

Sputtering and coughing up water, he could only watch helplessly as the giant ant reached out a leg and wrapped it securely around his chest.

Now Jaws had them both! Tears clogged Ryan's throat. He had tried so hard, but he and Raymond were doomed. Jaws was going to take them back to the dungeon at the bottom of the subterranean city to spend the rest of their lives digging tunnels. They would never get away.

Then he remembered Alex. He was still free. If only he could make it out and go for help! He was their only hope.

Suddenly Ryan noticed the ant had stopped. It wasn't moving downward anymore. Then, very slowly, it turned around and sloshed upstream.

Ryan's heart leaped. Was Jaws taking them to the entrance? Was it letting them go? Were kidnapped boys too annoying and rebellious, even for giant ants?

But an instant later his hopes were dashed. Jaws was making its way quickly over to Alex.

Alex had almost reached the top. He was stretching toward the light and scrambling as fast as he could toward the tunnel entrance.

But he froze as the giant ant's two middle legs reached out and clutched him.

Ryan thought his heart would break. Now everything was lost. All three of them had been captured again.

# Chapter

**J**aws turned and lumbered back down the tunnel with all three boys locked in its grasp. To make things worse, Ryan had dropped his tomahawk and Alex had lost his spear. They were totally helpless and defenseless.

Ryan frantically pulled and yanked at the leg that held him. But the ant's leg was as tough as a steel cable. He couldn't begin to loosen its grip. There was nothing to do now but await his fate.

"Ryan! M-M-My back pocket!" yelled a terrified voice.

He jerked around. Jaws had Raymond's arms pinned to his body, and Ryan had to look over his shoulder to see his brother.

"What? What are you talking about?" he said.

"The can!" Raymond yelled again. "Get the can! It's in my back pocket!"

Ryan could see something sticking out of his brother's pocket. He reached for it, but he could just barely touch it with the tips of his fingers. He shifted around in Jaws's grip and tried again. This time his fingers curled around it and he yanked it out.

Pulling it toward him, he couldn't believe his eyes. *Raymond had been carrying a can of ant spray in his pocket!*

Ryan knocked the lid off against the leg that held him just as Jaws lumbered to a stop. Looking down, Ryan could see that the passage was blocked by the enormous body of the queen. Ants were swarming around her, trying to get her back into her nest.

There was no time to lose. Ryan held the can as high as he could and squirted ant poison directly into Jaws's mouth.

The giant ant shook its head as if it was bewildered. Then it shook its head again and started digging at its mouth with its free leg.

Jaws staggered, dropping all three of the boys

at once as it stuffed its other three upper legs into his mouth.

Ryan dropped to the floor of the tunnel and landed next to the queen. Raymond hit the ground beside him. Then Alex bounced off the queen and rolled down on top of them.

Ryan scrambled loose and looked around frantically, expecting to be bitten in half by Jaws's giant pincers any second. Instead he saw the monster double over, trembling from head to foot.

All of a sudden the other ants seemed to sense that danger was near. They had forgotten the queen and were rearing up on their hind legs, waving their antennae in the air as they turned and twisted in all directions.

Suddenly two of them started climbing over the queen's body. They were heading straight for the boys. Ryan stuck out his arm and gave the first one a fast shot of bug spray right in the antennae. For an instant it was stunned. Then it whipped its feelers back and started scratching at them with its pincers and legs.

The second ant was reaching toward Raymond. Ryan gave it a squirt and shouted, "Come on. Let's make a run for it!"

"Ryan, help!" Alex cried shrilly.

Ryan looked back. An ant had Alex by the foot and was starting to drag him backward around the queen. Quick as a flash, Ryan ran to Alex and sprayed the ant. It dropped Alex's foot like a hot potato.

Then Ryan noticed Jaws. The big ant was lying still on the ground, and it looked as if it was dead. And the two ants that had tried to crawl over the queen and attack them were slumped on top of her, blocking the tunnel even more.

"Get going!" he yelled, pushing Raymond and Alex toward the opening to the outside.

"But what about you?" Raymond cried. "You're coming, too, aren't you?"

"Don't worry about me! Just get going!" Ryan insisted.

Alex and Raymond turned and ran, slipping and stumbling through the raging water toward the entrance to the mound.

When Ryan looked back down the tunnel, another ant was trying to squeeze past the queen to get to him. He waited until it had come halfway through the space left between the queen and the wall and then gave it a big squirt of ant killer. Its antennae curled back and it started rubbing its face with its legs. Finally it collapsed, further closing up the space between the queen and the tunnel wall.

The queen must have sensed the danger to the colony. She lifted her head and started trying to roll over. The ants on top of her were sliding off!

Ryan ran up to her head and gave three squirts—one for Alex, one for Raymond, and one for himself. The queen reared back and began to writhe and squirm, rubbing her head in the dirt.

Ryan turned and started climbing through the slippery tunnel toward freedom.

He was exhausted when he finally reached the entrance, but he couldn't stop. Rainwater gushed over him as he scrambled through the opening.

To his immense relief, Alex and Raymond grabbed his arms as soon as his head was out in the open and dragged him up. He rested a second and let the beautiful rain wash over him.

Daylight flooded his blinking eyes, and a

breeze softly stirred the rain-drenched branches of the trees.

"Are they coming?" Raymond asked nervously.

"I don't think so," Ryan said. "The spray worked. The tunnel's completely blocked with dead ants."

# Chapter

The boys got to their feet and headed down the hill.

"I just want to get home," Ryan said. "I bet Mom and Dad are mad!"

Raymond shook his head. "No, they're not. They're worried."

"So how come *you* found us?" Ryan asked. "And how come you had a can of ant spray in your pocket?"

Raymond grinned slyly. "When you didn't come home, everyone started to worry. I decided to go look for you myself. Then when I saw that huge anthill, I figured there must be a lot of ants in it, so I got my bug spray. I like ants, but that doesn't mean I like getting all bitten up."

"You know something? You *are* pretty smart," Ryan said, chucking Raymond on the chin with his fist. "If you hadn't gone back for the spray, we'd be dead meat and so would you."

Raymond smiled proudly. Suddenly he grabbed Ryan's arm and pushed him off the path.

"What are you doing?" Ryan yelled.

"It's a trail of ants," Raymond said. "Be careful!" He pointed at the place on the forest floor where Ryan had almost stepped.

The three boys looked down and saw a procession of small black ants, as narrow as a line drawn by a pencil. It wound its way across the footpath at their feet. Carefully, so as not to hurt a single ant, they moved to the side and continued silently home.

This collection of spine-tingling horrors will scare you silly!
Be sure not to miss any of these eerie tales.

# BONE CHILLERS

created by
**Betsy Haynes**

## BEWARE THE SHOPPING MALL
Robin has heard weird things about Wonderland Mall. When she and her friends go shopping, she knows something creepy is watching. Something that's been dead for a long time.

## LITTLE PET SHOP OF HORRORS
Cassie will do anything for a puppy. She'll even spend the night alone in a spooky pet shop. But Cassie doesn't know that the shop's weird owner has plans for her to stay in the pet shop . . . forever!

## BACK TO SCHOOL
Fitz thinks the food at Maple Grove Middle School is totally gross. His friends love Miss Buggy's cooking, but Fitz won't eat it. Soon his friends are acting strange. And the more they eat . . . the weirder they get!

## FRANKENTURKEY
Kyle and Annie want to celebrate Thanksgiving like the Pilgrims. Then they meet Frankenturkey! Frankenturkey is big. Frankenturkey is bad. And Frankenturkey may eat them for Thanksgiving.

## STRANGE BREW
Tori is bored stiff. Then she finds a mysterious notebook. Each time she opens it, a new spell appears, and strange things happen. Now Tori's having fun . . . until the goofy spells turn gruesome.

## TEACHER CREATURE
Everyone except Joey and Nate likes the new teacher, Mr. Batrachian–and he likes all the kids. In fact, sixth-graders are his favorite snack!

## FRANKENTURKEY II
When Kyle and Annie make wishes on Frankenturkey's wishbone, they bring him back to life. And this time, he wants revenge.

## WELCOME TO ALIEN INN
Matt's family stops at a roadside inn, only to find that the innkeepers are aliens eager to experiment on the first Earthlings that come their way.

## ATTACK OF THE KILLER ANTS
The school picnic is crawling with ants . . . so Ryan and Alex start stepping on them. And now a giant ant wants to drag them back to its monster anthill and make them slaves.

## SLIME TIME
When Jeremy sneezes, his snot suddenly takes on a life of its own–and the entire town is threatened by a tidal wave of slime.

## TOILET TERROR
Tanya decides to flush her failed science project down the toilet. But her brother had just flushed their dead pet goldfish. Something strange is brewing in those pipes . . . and it's ready to come out.